Brooke, Elisabeth

A February cuckoo

Elisabeth Brooke was born in Kent and has lived on several continents. She has written six books on subjects ranging from women's history and herbalism, to astrology and esoterica, including *A Woman's Book of Herbs* (The Women's Press, 1992), *Women Healers Through History* (The Women's Press, 1993) and *A Woman's Book of Shadows: Witchcraft – A Celebration* (The Women's Press, 1993). She divides her time between Fitzrovia and Santo Domingo, singing and playing the drums – she has no other vices. *A February Cuckoo* is her début novel.

Also by Elisabeth Brooke from The Women's Press:

A Woman's Book of Herbs (1992)
Women Healers Through History (1993)
A Woman's Book of Shadows: Witchcraft – A Celebration (1993)

A FEBRUARY CUCKOO

Elisabeth Brooke

First published by The Women's Press Ltd, 1997
A member of the Namara Group
34 Great Sutton Street, London EC1V 0DX

British Library Cataloguing-in-Publication Data
A catalogue record for this book is available from the British Library

ISBN 0 7043 4516 1

Typeset by The Harrington Consultancy
Printed and bound in Great Britain by BPC Paperbacks Ltd.

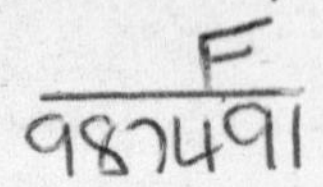

A FEBRUARY CUCKOO

Chapter One

She walks at night. In the empty places, the sad places. Paper blows past her feet, catches her. Lightly lifts her boots (always boots), she walks around the sleeping hungry. Looks through, piercing their souls, they groan and turn away. Her gaze, cat's eye misses nothing, slides past, will not meet you.

Shadows her world, daylight is alien land. She waits in corners, dark alleyways, foetid passageways. Watches cracks in the wall, the dripping pipe, the steady drunken progress of the cockroach on the kitchen floor. The swish and hum of meat wagons, swaggering cops dead-eyed, hears the sound of beatings, sights seen but not forgotten. Washed up dross shipwrecked on greasy streets, shop doorways; crumpled, bleeding, spewing, ejaculating, grinding away, teeth, dicks, fists. Clenching hands closing, buttocks. Doors slamming. None opening, the closed-eyed, dead-faced voracious consumer. Cars racing, tyres burning tarmac, exhausts belching.

Dead city, now rotting from the inside. Empty shop fronts gape, fly-posted, litter gathering in corners, coke tins, sweet wrappers, old newspapers. In the debris, shapes in filthy blankets wrestle for sleep in arctic cold, bitter wind. Malaise has spread crabwise through the city. The brash eighties imploded, services are abolished, cut, downsized.

Excess to requirements they sit and beg in fashionable streets, grimy, grey-faced, pinched with cold. Hungry eyes, sometimes hopeful, sometimes raging, soaked with terrible pain. The drink hides it briefly. Angry they spit and punch and roar their anguish, muffled as the city crumbles from want, neglect, despair and the avarice of a few. Corruption, the only healthy plant, feeds on sewer life, grows stronger, fecund, tensile, sucking the lifeblood as libraries close, schools decline, patients die in hospital corridors, alone, unattended, uncared for. The air is heavy with broken dreams, empty promises, shattered lives.

The city grinds on, lumbering, punch drunk. The bars and clubs overflowing as those that can, bump and grind and drink and smoke, embrace oblivion. Dealers prosper, cruise the city, sleek and menacing. Pimps and porno merchants offer tawdry escape, tantalising brief, putrid dreams.

Candida walks on, absorbing. She is out of the race, was never in, can watch dispassionate the glitter and the dross; she chases no paper tigers. Her strangeness repels, a great looming figure. She looks on but when addressed curls back into herself. Her shyness perceived as hostility, teased and bullied through school her defiance settled like concrete around her. Encased she is impenetrable and long ago stopped the struggle to fit in. The space was in any case too small.

Night-time wanderings bring her close to others on the edge. Night softens, blurs distinctions. The crazies, lost ones, spill out on to the streets from daylight bolt holes and wander looking for excitement, company, distraction. They gather in loose tribes around the bright lights, the best pickings, the tourist trail. They sit in huddles by the Hippodrome, Oxford Street, Leicester Square in damp sleeping bags. Pooling their takings they buy beer and cigarettes and watch with envy and contempt homegoing couples, wide-eyed tourists.

She stands with them on the outside, the one-eyed tramp greets her, they offer beer and cider and cigarettes. In the land of misfit she is citizen; they murmur, pass on scams and fiddles. Dream the deal that never was that will take them from this place. They remain nameless, theirs is a country where the past is razed and only the present matters. They accept her for her silence, her strangeness, and look out for her. She walks the streets unmolested.

She gathers people like the wind, catching falling leaves, pulls them to her and they walk. Laughing softly, heads bent, they gather in knots, whispering secrets, buying and selling. The panther, unseen, circles, guards them ferociously, snarls and spits, pads heavily, long, thick tail cutting the air as it moves from side to side. Black satin sheened coat glitters in headlights, catching moonlight in puddles, flashing, blinding passing tramps who stagger, curse, but do not spit. Taking a wide circuit they know. They know.

On cold nights and sultry evenings she brings them home and feeds them spoonfuls of warm soup, pitta bread and cashew nuts. She holds them close, crushing them until their bones crack and pop, enfolding them. Heating their frozen blood. They lie together on linen sheets and twist and turn, flesh meets flesh, she sucks them in, and greedily empties the bitterness from their marrow. White smoke rises to the ceiling, hovers. Beads of sweat condense, run along the walls, collect in puddles, the colours run. Books sigh and open, the clock ticks on, counting.

She snores when sleeping, open-mouthed, her hair a magenta stain on magnolia sheets, huge breasts proud and bursting, nipples red and swollen. Her skin ample, ocean-vast, white-grey of the city, dimpled lies inert, splayed, sated, her lover sleeps emptied, face pressed against her belly murmuring to himself. Their rhythm coalesces, sinking, rising, one heap of tangled flesh. Oozing, throbbing, limp.

Panther paces, restless, aching to be out, walking. Sinews cramped, he leans and stretches forward. His claws, catching the rug, dig into the varnished floorboards curving downwards, rump high tail heavy. He yawns, straightens up, curling his tail around his toes, spine erect. Gazes transfixed at the dust dancing in the sunlight.

Up and awake her lover dresses quietly, scans the room, pockets her purse and a silver teaspoon, spies a key and takes that too; she has been kind to him. In the kitchen he slices a wedge of cheese, eating it thoughtfully he slips out of the door, closing it softly, practised.

Stepping lightly, almost jauntily, he trails his fingers on the banisters, notices peeling paint, eggshell and the disinfectant smells of pissed-in corridors. Bedsit aroma of shop-bought pie and electric oven. Slams the outer door and turning, he looks up, blinks; a large cat with green-grey eyes leaning from a balcony watches him. Not with surprise, or indignation but a weariness which troubles him more than he can explain.

Chapter Two

Lighting a fag he moves down the street, eyes scanning left to right. Thin, he is thin and dark, his bones stick out, thin, broken glass; he is proud of his lines. The gauntness; his hollow, sinking eyes have the junkie's deadness. A cool death courses in his veins, bitterness may clog his arteries one day. He takes, never gives, he is a hard man. Small and wiry, built like a flyweight, there is no fat on him. Smooth line blended into muscles, tiny bones, slender fingers, neat feet. He trains and shadow boxes, can run a mile and jump fences, climb drainpipes. His eyes are like ferrets, darting, fixing, jumping, watching for small chances, missing bigger ones, always missing.

Afraid of being excluded he walks alone, not lonely. Dressed in black, he is the hard man. He steals, cons and sleazes his way, but keeps an iron fist clamped down on little feeling. Women want to heal his hurt, warm him, show him hope. Grimacing he knows the lie, there is none. Eat or be eaten, else the bastards will get you. Small-framed, he is mean, one too many blows reckoned him to get protected. Knives and guns are not enough; he trains and runs an hour each day, pounding sodden streets, windswept parks pushing each time further; building.

He clocks the street, a typical London hotchpotch. Her side, huge Victorian houses divided and divided into rooms, the paint flakes from plaster mouldings, dustbins crowd the garden. The other, a squat block of sixties' flats, wood panels discoloured, but tidy lawns, a hundred net curtains face the road; the door is heavy and has an intercom.

The street is flyblown with last night's leavings, beer cans, chip wrappers, a flaccid condom nestles in the gutter, the wing of a dead pigeon flaps mournfully. A group of them peck and pull at a greasy wrapper.

A fading daylight shows a car-packed street, drivers sitting vacant in a long, slow-moving queue. A motorbike roars, cyclists snake and weave between the lines. A mother with a pram stands nervously at the kerbside, waiting to cross. People walk bent under the bitter wind; it's raining, cold, February.

He turns left towards the High Street, red buses, green buses, orange buses are wedged together, the air thick with fumes, acrid, burning, poisonous. He wheezes and pulls his thin jacket across his chest. Asthma rattles his bones with its heavy puffing and reaching for air.

He stops under a railway bridge and opens the purse; inside is a deep blue scarab, plaster, a pound coin. She was as empty as he was. Contempt. He throws the purse away but keeps the scarab.

Jamming fists in jacket he jogs in the rain. Willpower keeps him breathing, the air is so toxic and damp. At the intersection there is no movement at all, cars hoot sporadically, listlessly; this is the evening ritual. Large crowds gather round the bus stops, queues have broken down. A bus arrives, they rush it, fighting to climb on. He stops running, the crowd thickens and walks across the road toward the tube. He walks from the road through the booking hall to the High Street. The winos are looking grisly, gangrenous legs, black and bloody wounds on their faces, urine soaked clothes; they sit grimly swallowing the daily dose. Crowds surge up the escalator, mingle, disperse. He leaves by the other exit and walks across the road.

Into the fruit market he saunters, watching. Two rows of stalls, covers wrestling against the wind. Grimy fruit, dusted by the road, sags heavily, sodden yet underripe, waxy. Poor cuts of meat in plastic wrap, flimsy clothes, nylons, fake satin sheen with brushed cotton nighties, socks five for a pound, boiled sweets, jellies. A feast for the poor, bashed tins, marrowfat peas, spam. An empty greyness. Sweets for the rotten teeth, winceyette against the damp. Chapped hands, coarse faces, unrelieved vista of cheap crap.

He spies one. In a crowd, talking, purse in hand, she stuffs it in her pocket. They collide. Startled, she tumbles. Crowd gathers, vultures. They pick her up. Brushing down the sad faded coat. Thick black mud spreads a dark stain. She begins to cry. Her face is powdered, apple blossom, her hair white, it was tucked under a turban but it has gone awry. A cabbage leaf has slipped into one of the folds like a feather, it pokes out. Righted, they sit her on the pavement. It begins to drizzle in earnest. Her red coat seems too large for her now, shrunken, its great bulk mocks her frailty. A man bends over her, wiping her face with a tissue, murmuring. A cry goes up. Her purse has gone. She looks accusingly at the crowd, they step back and look away, around, not at her. Angrily she struggles up, her stick a weapon now, she pushes them back, looks about the rubbish strewn road.

He relaxes; she thinks she dropped it. Crossing the street, he slips into a pub. The purse is full. In the gents he empties the money into his pockets; purse in the bin. Fifty quid. Enough for a while. Walking past the bar he pauses but carries on.

Outside the crowd has gone. The shuffling shoppers resume their sad progress. Baskets on wheels, scarved heads bowed, caps a blur in the rain. The old woman is talking to a copper, he towers above her listening, patiently, he looks young, unshaven, a colt.

Hailing a cab he speeds southwards. City a blur, darkness now, night lights shimmering, squishing of rain and tyre. The cab takes back streets across the park and into Portland Place. The traffic has thinned out, moving southwards it spins down Regent Street through Leicester Square, glittering now the lights sparkle. Trafalgar Square cutting down Whitehall over the bridge into Kennington, finally Brixton.

Out and into a dark street. He rings a door bell, no street scenes for him. Too leary. Up the stairs, two at a time. Door cracks open gun points out. Then wider; he is let in. Small fry, but safe. They measure out, neatly wrapped and he is gone. Not leisurely; too much weaponry; in and out. Not how it was once. Used to be social, skin one up, rap, tea, chat; social. Not now. Only money now.

He walks into the pub thick with smoke, a babel of voices, all nations, races. Finds a stool, lights up, drinks, sinking into a soft cloud of oblivion he cracks a smile, the first today as the rhythm catches him. He leans back, mellow now and allows the sunshine to dance with him.

They turn and watch the small man, man in black leaning back, both elbows on the bar gazing, a crooked grin across his face, distorted by the scar, ear to mouth. A thumping pounding base grinds the furniture into the concrete floor, figures blend and merge with the pall of smoke, voices rise above, the melancholy rhythm echoes and floods as figures stream in and out, weaving, drinking, smoking, flashing teeth, eager eyes. Rising and falling with the beat the din skewers them against the wall. Babylon.

Nervously, their hands feel for each other. Sweaty, they are afraid. They watch wide-eyed the cacophony of horror unfold before them. Fresh from a Gloucestershire field, mud still on their boots their shock is unnameable, complete. Waiting. They have been waiting all day. Waiting is what is required. In cafés, in damp squats, by railway bridges and now in this pub, they wait. One song ends and merges into another, their heads vibrate, chests tightened to wheezing with the beat, the endless, awe-ful beat.

They have given him all their money so there is nothing to do but wait. Sweating, their palms slide from each other, this, after all was all they had. Each other. They try to blend in, but their awkwardness, cheap clothes, nose rings, earrings, gives lie to their trying.

He is tall and fair, looks Scandinavian, solid, muscular body with a wide, golden face, green eyes and a tumble of red gold curls reaching down to his shoulders. He wears a thick green coarse fisherman's jersey and a heavy black donkey jacket. His hands are huge, puffy, the nails dirty and bitten. He looks like a farm worker and fisherman, or perhaps a baker. His bland face is fixed, trying not to catch the eye of anyone. He is ill at ease in this black place, a country boy. His girl is his opposite, small, dark pointed face. Her nose quivers nervously, her hands twist in her lap. She, too, is dressed in coarse wool, thick, ungainly, too hot for this pub. She smokes nervously, thin roll ups, and plays with the stud in her ear moving it around, pulling at it. She sighs with frustration loud, heartfelt, impatient.

Finally, their man comes in. Nervous, jerky movements a heap of excuses, apologies. Thin, he looks half gypsy, Romany perhaps. His hair black, sleek and shiny. It falls in large ringlets to his collar and down his back. His skin is olive. Wind tanned, flush of the outdoors. Broken veins on his cheeks and deep crevices in his skin age him. His eyes, hazel, are sharp, but cool. He smiles, 'I had a job, it's getting harder and harder. The Bill are nabbing people all over the shop. It cost more.'

The couple sigh, groan, there is no more money. 'There's no more!' They wail. 'No more, no more!' They sink back exhausted and terrified. Four eyes appeal to him.

'Okay, okay. But what am I supposed to do?' He faces them. They were new on the road, probably have savings, pensions, God knows what. 'Well, you'll have to owe me. Twenty knicker more.' He pushes over an envelope, holds their gaze. They have the hard bargaining of house people. He doubts they'll survive the winter. 'Twenty quid. Listen I had to pay up. Pay me!' His tone harder, threatening.

They look at each other. Perhaps they had been expecting this. The man reaches down, fumbles in his sock and produces the note. 'Cheers mate.' He takes it fast. One born every minute. And walks out of the pub whistling.

They open the envelope checking the precious documents, they were safe for another year. The bent MOT certificate would keep the bus on the road and they would be in it. They leave the pub arm in arm. Outside the dark night devours them.

Chapter Three

Slowly she unravels, legs from the sheets, mind from the dream. Sticky, sweating, she reaches over. The space is empty. She groans but is relieved, spared the after-conversation, empty of passion, the bored restlessness to escape. Plumping the pillows she lies back luxurious, and smokes. Her finger snakes down over her belly. Rubbing slowly the cat's eyes widen and then close, slits as it rolls and purrs, rolls and purrs.

Afternoon slides into night. Shadows pattern the peach walls, satin curtains glimmer iridescent, piled high they tower seductively, dangerously leaning. Dust softened the contours of the rocks and crystals meld into the shadows. Bleached driftwood, pine cones and flints gather on the tabletop, the mantelpiece a jumble of coloured postcards, feathers, dried flowers, rows of beads, earrings. Two vases, Chinese, carved red wood, a sprig of mistletoe left over, dried, the berries yellow and shrivelled. The fire glows softly in the darkness. Plants, their roots escaping with runners, tendrils, intertwined evergreen leaves, pale grey-green and white tips. Green, wavering fern, delicate, spreading, moist cheese plant, leaves dripping, newly born. High, long windows, thick with grime, look out down on to a wide road. Bamboo blinds pulled down, velvet curtains drawn. Candlelight plays with the shadows, blended with muted lamplight. She sits at her table, dressed now in soft wool and long flowing cotton covering huge breasts and buttocks. Feet in purple socks.

The cards turn. Spreading out the Celtic cross – past, present and future. White and gold they leap from the soft burgundy of the cloth: Hanged Man, Death, Temperance. The cat watches, impatient to go wandering, aching for night and out. Standing up she blows smoke across the room, incense burns, peppering the air with myrrh, juniper, laurel.

Her face is vast. Wide expanse of flesh, yellowish, colour of the night dweller. Her eyes brown and sad and dark, they hide beneath flesh; they pull you in sinking and drowning in some endless vat of treacle. Her mouth is small and tight, lips carmine. Amethyst twinkles from a nostril, jade from her ear. She eats slowly, feeding on jam and peanut butter, bananas, muesli, sips a mug of tea, crumbles cake, sweet and heavy, ginger.

As she eats she strokes a lizard carved from silken wood, its tail curled over. She'd loved insects and reptiles, played with the newts and frogs and toads from the pond. Their cool bodies fascinate, not slimy, dry. Feeling the pulsing, darting life in them, watching their tongues flick outward fly catching, bulging eyes, delicately webbed feet and toes, transparent pink nobs at the end of the web. Their tiny hearts beat as she held them, newts frozen, pretending to be rocks, bright eyes watching.

The pond was filled in by builders when she was eleven, the same year she'd been sent to her first shrink. The year she made her concrete shell and climbed inside. Through layers of fat she saw the world grow dim. She watched her frantic parents try to reach her, in the blood sugar high of chocolate cake. A girl in her class starved her way out, four stone and covered with suppurating bedsores, deaf to pleas and threats she died, tight-lipped. Candida munched pizza, drank milkshake and began to do deals to get the money to fund the binges. She found a 'man' in a dark pub basement and knocked out her quid deals in the respectable playground. They were all at it, uppers and downers, cough mixture, even nutmeg. Dealing gave her status and made her desirable, boys sidled up to her and stroked her cautiously, she bedded them serially; they were indistinguishable, pimply boys who quivered and shook, pierced her body but not the concrete, she remained intact but not ungrateful for the contact. They smoked her dope, talked about their girlfriends, and left without a thought. She took her food stealthily up on the hill behind the town, at home eating was policed, and ate and cried, ate and cried until she felt nothing and was restored.

Like limescale the layers piled on, imperceptibly, relentlessly she creaked like a rhino inside, tough hide, wrinkled, thick. Life had been simplified: food and some sex. All in her control, packets of lust, episodes of greed. She had no expectations, hope walled-up long ago. She looked not at horizons; but downward getting through the day was enough. Her compulsion was movement, to be out, walking and watching. People hardly figured: as long as there was someone it didn't matter who or what they said, just needed a vague proximity from time to time to stop her dissolving into herself. She didn't care much either. Had once, but disappointments hardened her, she got nothing, expected nothing except the most superficial contact.

Out! She takes the cloak of heavy black wool, lace-up boots, flesh dripping over edges. Mittens, no fingers. Black velvet hat, twinkling, sparkled with sequins which fell sometimes and glowed on her cheeks. She paints carmine lipstick on her lips and kohl around her eyes. Checking: bag, some loose change, knife. They leave; her first, the panther following along the concrete corridor down stone stairs. Evening cooking smells linger. TV sounds, voices low.

Out, the chill air rushes them, hurrying heads down until blood pumps warmer, faster than frozen damp. Winding past the bridge under and out, before the train clattered and shook the rotten brickwork. Lights flash, a few late shops trying to entice the cold and hungry. Turning left they pass the market, empty now. A woman with a stick and muddy turban pushes through the debris, rotting, sodden, filthy.

'Keep that cat away from me!' she threatens. 'Dirty, ugly great thing.' They veer off and leave her standing, watching grimly. She spits and turns. Back to the putrid gutter.

Rain has splattered fur down flat, ugly patches matt on gloss mark time with feline rhythm. Wet cloak leaks an essence, patchouli mixed with damp wool. Picking up speed she crosses the park, Inner Circle, she smiles wryly, the only inner circle she'd ever enter.

Two runners puff white mist as they pass on the other side; a cyclist peddles vainly against the building wind, the rain heavy; ice needles push from behind, moving them forward. Across the Marylebone Road into Fitzrovia they see Great Portland Street station, lit up, deserted now and the great slab of a church. Down toward the tower they pass the security patrol who stop and stare after them; the man makes a remark, the woman laughs a screeching laugh. They cross Oxford Street into Soho where street life hums, pubs and restaurants full, clubs pounding out a deep monotonous rhythm.

She stops in Old Compton Street and drinks a cappuccino, spooning the foam and chocolate powder, and orders cake, passion fruit. It is soft and moist warm under the lamps, thick cream icing, little nuts; sweet, perfectly sweet. The waitress looks disgusted as she orders a second; Candida smiles as sickly as the cake, her teeth streaked with butter fat. Triumph, she will not behave as nice girls do. Fuck them. She eats quickly, jumpy now and leaves. Past the theatre into Covent Garden, Seven Dials and down and along into the piazza.

They pause a while in the square, lit up now, floodlights picking out cornices, columns, twirly bits. They shelter under a balcony and watch diagonal lines of water fill puddles and galleys and run off into swollen drains. Rain has scattered casual wanderers. Kids have left their doorways. Filthy blankets lie discarded in shit-smeared doorways. Even paper cannot roll, sodden it lies flattened pasted downward. Exhausted.

Across the square a man comes walking, head up, oblivious in the rain. Thin and tall, anorexic, late middle age, poor, a tattered once-good suit, shoes scuffed, worn at the heel, tan briefcase and a pile of books stuffed under one arm, papers flapping. The rain has made his spectacles impossible, they are pushed onto his forehead and he leans forward trying to see through the lashing water. He, too, makes for the shelter and coming into view smiles at the two large figures as he strides into dryness.

Inside he shakes the rain away in a compulsive gesture. 'Hold these, will you?' offering out his books and case. She takes them, and looks down, curious. But she cannot read the writing, thin, spiky, running where the rain has splashed. She bends to put down the briefcase. He stops her, shouting, 'No! No! Hold it. Keep it dry. Don't put it down.'

She watches him resentfully as he takes out a cloth and carefully wipes the rainbows from his glasses. Slowly, methodically polishing them. They are gold-rimmed and round, he shines them and puts them on.

They examine one another. His eyes widen as he takes in the panther and narrow as he gazes above and beyond her head. 'Aura's muddy dear, needs cleaning.'

She stretches out her hand instinctively for the magic cloth.

'No, no, not with that. No. Not at all!' He laughs, patronisingly.

He stares some more. 'And there's a hole there.' She and the cat look up alarmed as he points to a place shoulder height. They look at one another and smile.

They watch in silence; the girl is not used to speaking. She stretches out as if to stroke him. He jumps back alarmed. And watches her again. Not sure now, is she safe? Is her madness contagious? The cat is very big. But even the most unlikely seed can blossom. Swallowing he moves in.

'Alone? Alone are you? This city is a lonely, dangerous place. Mmm. Lonely, dangerous,' he falters. The cat, restless now the rain is easing, begins to pace; circle and pace. Gathering his books he takes her arm. She pulls back alarmed. Panther comes closer, tail swings, a faint hiss escapes his razor teeth.

He is pulling her away from the shelter into the rain. Panther watches softly, muscles tightening arches high. Unsure he passes behind, tail low lying, belly scraping cobblestone. They move down through the plaza. Past the frock shops, florists, gaudy bookshops around the Seven Dials, painted hoardings, descending into traffic, swirling red, gold, green lights dazzling neon. They both pull back, but curiosity drives them on – he looks harmless, after all. Running now, people stopped to watch the odd couple, dodging traffic.

He doesn't have a house, she might have guessed. He leads her across the gusting bridge, arched over the boiling river. Slashing their faces, ripping their clothes, rain tears at them. Heads down, they progress unevenly. Cat growls softly, resentful. Along the other side the smell of woodsmoke marks the boundary.

In the tunnel, dark shadows hang menacingly on the slime-ringed walls. The stench hits them like a barrier. A dog runs across their path, turns and barks. Cat opens one eye. The dog yowls and flees. Curious, a hairy matted man/boy gets up from the fire he is tending. Bearded, pierced, he watches carefully. Bitten fingernails clasp a can. The dog runs behind him. Young, barely formed like his owner, its pepperpot snout quivers. Nothing is said.

A man is moaning, and rhythmically banging his head against the wall. Blood mingled with soot cascades down his face. A woman, a bundle of rags, runs to him and pulls him away cursing. They stagger into the tunnel.

A whey-faced girl, sullen and very thin, rises from the darkness. Clutching herself, she pulls at her clothes as if infested. Her face, grimy, has scabs and a swollen eye which fixes on them.

'Evening, Miranda,' he cheerfully calls to her.

She looks blank then disappointed. 'Money, give me money. I need money.'

He stops and turns to her. 'You'll only spend it on that filthy stuff; come and eat something.'

A faint glimmer of a smile, which quickly vanishes. 'No, money, I need money.'

This has the feel of an ancient ritual. The girl drifts off. They stop beside a wooden wardrobe lying on its side. Cardboard and rags lie on top. He opens the door and extracts a soot-blackened kettle.

'Sit, please sit.' He walks off with the kettle.

They sit, or rather she does. The cat is uneasy and paces, forward, around, from side to side. They know these places. She fears them. People with nothing. Distress, bombed-out brains, no-hopers. Vigilance. The smell was bad. Acrid smoke filled the tunnel, drifted away, lethargic. The whole place languorous, apathetic, slow. Aroma of despair, defeat, angry capitulation.

They sit so long she wonders if he has forgotten them. Gazing unfocused she avoids curious eyes. Sniffing dogs keep away. The panther paces. Eventually he returns with two mugs, steaming. 'Sugar? No? Just as well as there is none. Biscuit?'

He opens his briefcase and extracts two salami sandwiches, egg and bacon, tuna and mayonnaise, fudge cakes wedged in stiff cellophane. Bananas, pears, small cartons of orange juice. Chocolate bars. Salivating wildly, Candida reaches forward, takes the cheese and pickle on rye and rips off the cellophane wrapping, then crams them double into her mouth.

'Liberated food,' he offers. 'Naturally you are wondering how such a refined and cultivated man finds himself here in this hell hole of misfits and human debris.' She hadn't. The stories were usually the same. Fractured relationships, loss of job/money, lack of friends/the street.

'I am here on a mission of mercy. I work with these poor unfortunates.' She bristled at his patronising tone, yet felt pleasure in not being included.

'I am bringing them truth. Truth and light.' He takes out a card and offers it to her. She takes it. On it is written:

Bill Wilson
your problems solved through prayer
Seek and ye shall find.

'Are they interested?' she asks sarcastically.

He ignores the question, she continues eating. Watching him, his neck stiff with bogus dignity surveying the chaos which surrounds him. He jerks abruptly, a nervous twitch. Bored, she examines him; his fingernails are long, his hands delicate, his suit shiny and with a stain that looks like egg on one lapel, his tie is red and crumpled and the shirt creased grey. She sighs; lonely and mad. Was there no one else other than the lonely and mad?

On her third Mars bar she pauses, gagging. A very pregnant rat saunters past, big, almost kitten size. The dog flies at it, barking exultantly. The rat turns and faces its tormentor. Glittering eyes, bared, yellow fangs, tail flashing it leaps, paws outstretched, and sinks its fangs into the dog's soft throat. Howling with pain, the dog bends and twirls and frantically shakes its neck, but the rat hangs on.

A thin stream of blood arches out and patterns the wall. A drop falls on her wrist. She looks at it, pale red, drying crusty. Getting up she clears the wardrobe before she vomits. Cheese and pickle, salami on rye, three Mars bars. The cat watches the sinking dog with a warm satisfaction.

A boy appears from the shadows and tries to batter the rat with a burning plank, but they are both beyond help. Collapsing on the floor, bright red blood on black fur. Grey lump, serpent tail. Bashing frenziedly, the rat, too, begins to bleed. The boy, caught in a timeless blood lust, thumps until a twitching mass of fur and blood and entrails lies steaming on the floor.

Outside, the dark night mocks Candida and the cat. In this otherworld the neon sign flashes on and off. Taxis chunter past, a train rattles on the overhead iron bridge. No echo of the bleeding terrors in the tunnels. Toytown. A drunk in a suit wanders abstractedly, trying to hail a taxi.

They plough the route back across the bridge, both dispirited. The blood has dried on her hand. She pulls on a mitten. They lean a while on the bridge, gazing down at the water, standing together. The cat nuzzles her; she takes his head in her hand and holds it close, firmly. His warm rhythm calms her. Uncomplicated, feline, instinctual. He purrs, deep, rasping, ancient. She cries, misery overwhelms her, bitter tears run. They drop into the water and are carried, rushing toward the sea.

In the morning she wakes and, turning, feels his body. Puzzled she tries to remember. All she can see is blood and fur and the transfixed delight of the boy hitting, mashing, pulverising animal flesh. Leaning up on her elbow she looks at him. Small, muscular, a scar runs across his face. Nondescript, ratty around the edges. Poor, working-class kid, bad food, too many blows. He winces in his sleep. Mean hair, sparse, badly cut. Cheap gold earring. Surprisingly slim fingers and small hands, neatly cut fingernails, shell pink. Sinewy body, boxer? Petty crook probably. Dishonest but not dangerous. She has yet to miss her purse.

He lies with his eyes closed, breathing softly. He can feel her watching. He swells, imagining her satisfaction and delight at the treasure in her bed. His body sculpted, perfect in its way, responds to her attention. Glad he had taken the key, he let himself in just before dawn. Full of the goodwill of marijuana. He rolls on top of her smiling grimly, and quickly, meanly, fucks her.

A deep sigh whistles through her teeth. Miserable grief like a fog gathers around her bruised heart. Sated, he smiles, triumphant. Leaning back she aims her massive thigh and kicks him out of her bed and onto his discarded clothes.

The cat springs up, eyes narrowing, crouches ready to pounce. Last night's blood has whetted his appetite. He relishes the thought of a few deep slashes in such tender flesh. The man stands naked, lip trembling.

'Why did you do that?' He looks hurt, vulnerable.

She beckons, he creeps back under the sheets. She holds him and they drift off again. He tries in a halfhearted kind of way. Leaden now, her heart drops to the bottom of a well; resting in soft mud she sleeps again.

The afternoon light filters through the blinds, strips and thin lines on the worn carpet. She wakes heavy, dull-witted and alone. Again she is thankful. The cat sits with its back to her in a pointed, offended manner. A fly is trapped between the glass and the blind, it buzzes, irritated, banging against the glass. Again and again. Again and again. The cat studies the sound but guesses the prey not worth the effort and remains obelisk still.

Smoking, she sees the dog, the rat, the boy. Hunger and nausea jostle. Hunger wins by force of habit. The pall of disappointment remains, but it is familiar. She pads to the kitchen, loads the tray. A special kind of food is called for, treat/baby food. Peanut butter, crunchy, no sugar, pear and apple spread, rice cakes, hummus, crunchy garlic, corn chips, cashews, chocolate mousse: individual, two avocados: ripe, oily, orange juice in a carton. Settling against the pillows she notices the cat has not moved, his ears are pinned back with disapproval.

She calls him. Silence. Again, no response, he does not like her men. She sighs and scoops up a dollop of hummus with corn chip. Salty, garlic. Another and another. Acid rebels in her stomach. Slicing the avocado deftly unpeeling a quarter slice she mashes it into a rice cake, liberally sprinkled with black pepper. It lines her stomach. More hummus, then hummus and avocado together, sweet and spicy. The cat is still. But bending an ear an improbable 180 degrees listens to her eating.

Sometimes the food doesn't work. Sometimes. She puts the tray to one side. Cat, rat, dog, boy. It will not leave her. She picks up a slipper and throws it at him. He jumps aggrieved to one side, with what looks like a sardonic smile. Stretching out a hind leg he runs his tongue up and down his black glossy fur. She throws the other slipper. He totters and canters on to the bed. Nuzzling and nipping, dipping a pink tongue into the hummus, wrinkling with distaste. They cuddle up. Forgiven.

She feeds him licks of mousse, he buries his face and jerks his head up under her chin. She strokes and holds his quivering body close.

Chapter Four

☾

The door bell wakes her. She had drifted off with the cat, curled up foetal, side by side. It rings again, a third time, insistent. She crosses the room and pulls back the blind. From the reflection of the window opposite she can see a woman standing at her door. Woman with a briefcase. Official. She pushes up the window and shouts down, 'Yes?'

The woman looks up. A worn harried face of an overworked social worker lifts towards her. 'Housing,' she says curtly.

'Oh,' replies Candida flustered. 'I'll be down in a minute.'

Throwing her cape over her nightie, she goes downstairs. Opening the door, a thin, tired woman walks past, taking charge.

This, this way.' Candida half-leads, half-follows as the woman bolts up the stairs.

They sit down. 'Housing' notices with alarm the tarot cards still spread on the table top. Officiousness fails to mask her apprehension,which fills the room.

Just a routine check to . . . she trails off. Panther has sidled up to her. She looks around in vain for the cause of her confusion, but sees nothing.

'Proof of identity.'

'Eh?'

'Do you have proof of identity?' Struggling to retain control.

'Er, well,' Candida gazes hopelessly at the mess in the room. Several weeks have passed since she had last tried to wrestle order out of the paper chaos; she needs help to sift the vital from the ephemeral.

Recently there has been no one. She's withdrawn into the darkness inside her. Autistic, mute, she's had little to say or do with others. The strange man in the suit and the man in her bed have been the only contact, but it has hardly been verbal. They'd talked at her, failing to register or comment on her silence. They were not bill sifters in any case. Takers not givers.

Her silence is a fix to her. An indulgence which became a necessity sometimes. Winter was hard, life on the streets diminished. Her people, such as they were, retreated into the septic tunnels or out in lorries into the country, playing hide and seek with the police. She wonders if she will become one of the mad women who shout at lamp posts or sit crumpled on park benches, gazing empty-eyed, brain fried by thorazine.

Housing closes her eyes, hoping that when she opens them she might be anywhere but here. Knowing how rarely her wishes were granted she sighs heavily. 'A passport, driving licence, bank book?'

Candida has none. She shrugs and looks appealingly at the woman. Her shame at her ignorance makes these official visits a nightmare. She feels the growing exasperation of the woman and pities her, yet she is helpless.

'I don't drive or fill in forms unless someone helps me. I'm sorry, I'm sorry, I'm not trying to annoy you, I can't help it you see . . .' Blubbering now, tears run down the familiar rivulets, staining the crimson of her nightdress.

The woman sighs again. This is the first call of the day; she has another ten to make. Bloody hell, bloody hell! Why does she always get the crazies? It is so unfair. She isn't a bloody social worker, nor, eyeing Candida suspiciously, a psychiatric nurse.

'Do you have a social worker?'

Candida remembers and gives her her name.

'Well, I'll talk to her then.' She slaps her file shut, delighted. And is up and out before Candida can move.

Downstairs the door slams. From the window Candida and the cat watch her cross the road. Thick and stupid! Thick and bloody stupid. That's what she is, thick and bloody stupid! A wave of the past crashes through her. Taunting children, coldly sarcastic teachers, numb confusion and hopelessness faced with hieroglyphics on the blackboard. She second guessed the answers and was right often enough that they let her be. Or perhaps tired of the game. Stupid and fat. That too. In such a sleek and intelligent family. A changeling, yet with enough of their features not to beg the question. The last of four. Three brave, hearty, well-adjusted English children. And then her, Candida. They'd even laughed at her name. Candied peel. Hopeless. In the face of such perfection rebellion was the only route. Her fat was that. Eating and growing, then eating and growing more, then eating and growing more, and still more and more. She had split her seams, burst out of her neatly pressed shirts, waddled helplessly along hockey pitches. Sat in gymnasia sweating, popping buttons, revelling in her defiance of perfect siblings, whose sleek muscled forms trampolined, cartwheeled and hopped, jumped and skipped through their childhoods.

They had swept through the best the Home Counties could offer and on to safe secure professions, respectable marriages, glowing parenthood; the siblings were a united front in their efforts to redeem Candida. The more they nagged and teased the firmer her will became. Candida the baby became Candida the gross. She sat buddha-still, immobile and deaf to their pleadings. When adolescence came and Candida gave a final, obese growth spurt they gave up. Afraid their friends might meet such a misfit, they avoided mentioning parties and picnics when she was there.

Psychologists were called for by her vexed parents. A series of bald patronising old men made futile attempts to reach her, one even recklessly sat her on his knee, but she remained silent, oafish and resigned. Closed off, alone, buried by acres of flesh. Candida found friends, phantoms. The more dependable of which was the panther, which grew more and more real as her family faded.

Later, when she heard about witches and their familiars, she wondered if the cat was that. A devilish apparition, evil sprite, who promised pacts with old Nick in return for supernatural powers. The cat remained but no devils materialised and she noticed that the mad and the drunk could see it too. They watched uneasily his great shining black torso. Stepped back when he lay belly low and snarled. Warmed to his purring. This reassured her, that although she might be mad she was not the only one.

She drifted from her family, gradually and undramatically; she had no friends. They seemed relieved that she absolved them and cut loose. There were some phone calls, which came less and less and the occasional cheque took the place of parental interest.

Moving into squats she found people like herself, the babblers and the mumblers, no hopers and rich kids slumming, the lost and forlorn rubbed shoulders with the hard-eyed junkies and the paranoid dealers. They casually took her into their lives and as casually dropped her, as squats closed and opened, people busted or died, went straight or moved on. She liked the rolling changes of these people. No questions asked, no need to shine, impress, talk even. Hot tea, munchies for the dope heads and the occasional fiver for the destitute was enough love, spread thinly for all who wanted it.

Women trusted her and talked without listening, rolling paper-thin fags and drinking mug after mug of strong, dark tea. Some even stroked the cat absentmindedly as they sat by the fire. Men stroked her. The boyish ones sought out her fleshy expanses. On cold nights they bedded down, but were gone as spring approached, after finer flesh.

Life passed uneventfully, wave after wave of people, getting younger now. A Frenchwoman taught her to read the cards, pointed out the Empress, the Magician, Judgement. Candida learned, eagerly she understood the markings as if from another time, and now she survived on her readings, built up a clientele, which kept her comfortably, and gave her the deposit for the flat she was forced to find when finally all the squats ran out.

She couldn't remember where the social worker had come from, perhaps her parents had sent her, or maybe she was a client. But she had been a long-standing feature in her life who popped up at irregular intervals, usually in need of tea and sympathy, not giving it.

Brushes with authority still bring back the pain of her childhood, the stigma of her dyslexia, the bungled attempts to reach out, the threats, blackmail and ostracism. The tears flood out, pity, anger, fear. She is wiping the last ones away when the door creaks open; she and the cat watch as the thin man lets himself in.

He is even more furtive than she remembers, and shabbier. He sees her and swaggers unconvincingly, knowing she has seen his vulnerability. She remembers it is winter and sighs. Till March then? He looks broke and half-starved, her heart opens like a petal and she smiles pityingly. He pecks her on the cheek; 'Any food?'

Chapter Five

In the tunnels the smoke is thick and suffocating, blown in by an icy north wind. Bill sits on his wardrobe ruminating. It had been hard last night. They had removed the bodies, the tangled flesh of rat and dog. But the boy remains distraught, raving. Now he is wandering to and fro in front of the wardrobe. Pacing, muttering. Dressed in khaki fatigues and thick-toed boots he is the parody of a young soldier. His eyes glittering, his movements jumpy, sharp-tipped, expecting anger, hurts, insults.

Thoughts stab his mind. They hurt. A thousand tiny razor cuts have slashed his brain, disconnected it is oozing, caking and cracking as he rots from the inside out. Maggots squirm ferocious, nibbling, chewing, salivating as they consume his brain flesh. He shudders trying to dislodge them. But they were put there long ago, by his father, who told him he was offal, tripe, trash. He beat him with belts, slippers, and, latterly, his fists. That was when the flies got in and laid the maggots, when his nose was split and his eye busted as his daddy stood over him telling him to take it like a man. His beating. Like a man. He rolled over, to shield his face, took one in the kidneys and lay inert. His mum was crying, useless, empty tears. Worried he might start on her next. She watched but never tried to stop him. He guessed they both agreed about the rottenness, the maggots.

He'd left soon afterwards when the flies began to buzz instructions to him, telling him to stab and slice, to kill and kill and kill. Last night he had, and the blood appeased them: they stayed.

Now though, they have begun again, whispering, urging him. He is afraid.

Bill studies him. His young face is screwed up in panic, deep lines gouge his forehead, his eyes bright, hard. The kid is cracking up in front of him, Bill can almost see him cracking cell by cell. The old man wonders how he can reach him, and if he dares or even wants to. Watching him pacing is unbearable.

'Come! Come and sit with me a while. Let me get you something,' he calls out across the abyss, but his voice fades. The boy continues to move as if the words have not reached him. Suddenly he stops. Turns around, looking for the place the voice has come from. The old man smiles hopefully, doubtfully; the boy's eyes are empty of reason and sweep past him as though he were a lamp post or a brick in the wall. He continues pacing, grinding his teeth and muttering bitterly to himself. He is begging the flies to stop, just for a while. And they do, mercifully they fade.

He stands still and it seems for the first time sees the crumpled dingy old man sitting watching him. He seems concerned, frightened, wary. 'Hi!'

Bill watches, perplexed, but replies, 'Hello, cup of tea?'

'Oh yes, yes, tea, tea would be, be . . .' he trails off, unsure what tea would be. Tea/be, tea/be, the rhyme reminds him of the flies, he shivers and crosses both sets of fingers.

'Tea, sandwich perhaps? I believe there's one left.' The old man has no appetite after last night's slaying and in any case makes a point of not eating stale food. He rummages in his briefcase. 'Cheese and pickle suit you?'

The boy takes it gingerly and looks at it dubiously wondering if there are maggots in the cheese or slugs in the lettuce. He puts it carefully in his pocket. He will examine it later, outside where the light is better. He sits down on the wardrobe and suddenly feels agonisingly tired and lies down, awkwardly balancing on the pile of rags which smell of woodsmoke, old socks and an undefined animal. He sleeps.

When the old man returns with two mugs of tea the boy is curled up precariously, sleeping. He feels irritated. He's cadged the boiling water from the foetid couple further down after much discussion as to its value and their inconvenience. And now the boy sleeps. But he guesses it won't be for long, he is twitching and seems to be shaking something off him.

An aching, lonely tenderness fills him as he watches the boy. The old man is new to the tunnel and has not boned up on everyone. In any case, past lives are little discussed. He is here on a mission, or so it seems, it is only temporary. Soon enough he will be out of here. Soon enough. He leans forward to catch the sandwich as it slides out of the boy's pocket and carefully balances it on top of the tea.

He sips his tea, it is bitter without sugar. The boy makes him feel old, worn out. What has happened to the years is unclear. Too many corners cut and compromises made. A dingy, threadbare life full of boarding houses, stewed cabbage, betting slips and disappointments. Yes, those more than anything. Not enough good times, too much boredom and waiting about. Yes, waiting, waiting for the good times. Which never came or were so fleeting that he didn't notice them until they had slipped past him. Chimera, those good times, phantoms.

The boy stirs and shivers, the river damp is rising and night breaking in. He groans and opens his eyes, wild, searching and sits up. The flies are back, buzzing, frenzied and dive-bombing inside his skull.

'Here, it's getting cold.'

A waxy hand proffers a tin mug, steam rising gently from inside. The boy examines it, baffled.

'Tea, it's your tea.'

He looks up searching for the face that goes with the voice; an old man smiles faintly.

'Take it, drink it while it's hot.'

The boy takes the mug and looks into its russet depths. Doubtfully he takes a sip. Warm and bitter, there is no sugar, but good. He grins sheepishly at the face and swallows the rest. It heats him to a little above freezing. The flies drone softly now, drunkenly. The old man sits beside him, leaning forwards. He creaks and rustles like a tree. He is pretty old, looks kind, not dangerous, like a grandfather on TV.

The man passes him a Mars bar. It is safe, pre-wrapped. He tears the paper off it and eats, ravenously. Then looks for more. 'No, not the sandwich, more chocolate?'

But the man shakes his head. 'All gone, all gone.' Then pathetically, 'Sorry.'

The boy's eyes harden, sensing weakness, vulnerability. 'Got a fiver you can lend us? Pay you back?'

Again the man shakes his head. 'No luck, no. I'm afraid I don't have any to spare.'

'Not even a fiver. Come on!'

The man looks away. 'If I had money I wouldn't be here, would I?' he mutters.

'No, no, I guess not. Sorry.'

The flies are starting again. The boy gets up and walks past the man as if he is invisible and, catching up his coat, walks out into the night.

It is raining. He turns the corner and ducks into the tube station. The guard looks the other way as he leaps the barrier. He takes the Northern Line to Charing Cross. Here, shoppers laden feel guilty and give fifty pence, sometimes a quid. Men too sometimes, men in suits, guilt or fear, a kind of insurance against the same thing happening. Easy to slip, no one was safe, the gutter has no preferences.

'Spare any change? . . . Spare any change, please? Change?'

He is lucky, maybe it is payday, the stars right, whatever, he soon has enough. He takes the train north, Leicester Square, slips through again, and out into the night.

Food first. He has a ravenous hunger and makes for the café. They are faggots, might meet someone there, get a free meal, a bed. Though probably not, but company at least. Some nice guy. They know him there and feed him, chat to to him like he is human, when the place isn't too busy. He walks up Charing Cross Road and crosses under the great phallus of Centre Point.

The café is painted green and pink and perched at the edge of the terrace dwarfed by the skyscraper. The window is steamed up, he guesses it will be quiet. He opens the door expectantly.

Inside it is empty, only Ricardo sits behind the counter, whispering on the phone. He looks up and smiles as the boy hovers by the door and gestures him in. There is lots of left-over food and Ricci piles his plate steaming high, macaroni, sauce, bread, bottle of beer. It was quiet, a Monday night and the barman sits down with him as he eats. They know each other slightly. He talks and the boy listens. He likes these guys, soft but strong somehow, not like the straights. Strange, funny, gentle but on the fringes like him, marginal types, wary looks behind the bravado. They know what a pink triangle had meant, still does in some places.

The heat, the beer and the food make him drowsy again. Reeling he tries to concentrate but cannot follow what the guy is on about. He gives up the struggle and conks out.

'Hey! I'm not that boring am I?' Ricardo shakes him gingerly, aware his clothes are filthy. He feels for the kid, wishes there is something he can do. But there isn't. 'Okay, okay come on now! You can't crash out here!'

The boy opens his eyes and looks pleadingly at him, guessing it won't work. 'Yeah, yeah, I'm going. Don't panic!'

He pauses to consider if he should offer to pay, but feels bruised and resentful. Usually he can spend a few hours here, in the warm, safe.

Their eyes meet, the barman seems to relent and, exasperated, says, 'All right! All right! I get you some coffee, but don't fall asleep on me!'

The boy sleeps leaning in a darkened corner, snoring softly, his coffee going cold. The barman watches him, feeling frustrated and tender: little children, children in the cold. Tears prick his eyes, such a hard place, such a cold place, this. It is hard to remember the chain of events which led him to leave a tropical warmth of palms and guava for this concrete coldness. Hard to remember. But scars told their own stories. The long jagged one raised and puckered on his arm where the baton had smashed down and ripped his flesh, peeled it like a banana. And the ringing in his ears, which has never left him, the blow of the boot. He was lucky not to have died. At least he thought he was lucky. But his hearing is fuzzy on that side, he needs to turn to listen with his other ear, an endearing sideways motion of the head. As though he is leaning down to kiss or whisper. Luckier still he is young and pretty, his body still holds, his face not too drawn and pinched. And his teeth are good.

It had hotted up, one of the military had had a crush on him. Dangerous; such sweet boys, once tired of, tended to pass down through the ranks or disappear entirely. Hard to imagine in such a town as this, everything seemed so safe and predictable in comparison. They called it toytown, the other Latinos, both derisory and incredulously. Nothing they had ever known had been so cosy.

An older man comes in and interrupts his thoughts. He orders coffee and lemon meringue pie. His eyes are cool grey, his suit charcoal, immaculate, expensive, out of place. His tie is orange-red with what looks like a fish head design. He is possibly fifty and has an air of someone accustomed to power, who never needs to raise his voice. He pays with a crisp twenty-pound note and sits down opposite the sleeping boy.

There is something reptilian in his manner as he carefully forks the yellow pie and white-brown meringue into his red mouth. He watches the boy carefully, like a lizard watching a housefly. Examining him, turning him over in his mind, imagining how he will taste, salivating slowly. The musty odour of unwashed clothes troubles him; he frowns with distaste.

Feeling a predatory eye, the boy wakes and their eyes meet. Cool grey to milky black. Old to young, powerful to powerless. They understand one another perfectly. The boy smiles and rubs his eyes. He would like a bath, long, warm and scented. Clean linen, sound sleep.

'Can I get you something?' The man raises an eyebrow.

'I'd like a drink,' the boy counters.

'Well then . . . ' The man waits.

Collecting his coat and taking care not to look left or right or at Ricardo, the boy sashays out into the night.

'Let's go home, more comfortable,' the man says as he hails a taxi.

The door slams and they speed off. Ricardo watches, troubled, and then, sighing, clears away the boy's full coffee cup, gone cold. Settling down behind the bar again he picks up the phone and forgets them both.

Chapter Six

Bill stands in the queue behind the supermarket. They are giving away food. Food past its sell-by date. That amuses him. He is past his sell-by date too, well overdue. Usually it is sandwiches, sometimes pies and pasties, quiches, less often cheese, cakes, biscuits. Tonight there is salami, brie with walnuts, a cheese pasty, chocolate fudge cake, milkshake. Putting them in his briefcase, he walks off towards Covent Garden.

On fine nights he likes to sit in the piazza on one of the benches in front of the actors' church and eat his supper. Gingerly he looks up, the sky is starless but not threatening. He whistles softly as he walks south, crossing the cobbled side streets of Soho and into Seven Dials. Taking one of the streets that fan off from the monument he reaches the piazza and heads toward his favourite spot.

He chooses to face south toward the Strand, although it cannot be seen from the square. The buildings are high and white, calm, stately, secure. To his right is the African club, faintly he can hear strains of marimba, drums, laughter. People pattering in and out. To his left and behind the Rock club a different beat, lower, monotonous, mindless. Fighting sometimes breaks out in the street outside.

The golden hand crosses the cobalt face and clicks solidly. He peels open a packet, brie and walnut. Food is food, but this creamy crunchy mix is not altogether to his liking. He eats it anyway, and sits back. Disagreeable and uncomfortable, sometimes dangerous, life on the street has a *frisson* that bedsitting never knew about. You meet people. Yes, they are strange and bad but they don't judge, in the harsh relentless way ordinary people judge. Standards are basic. People are concerned with self-protection, reticence, caution, and have an inverted pride; they are passionately defensive of themselves and their lives. The weak die or leave the streets, self-pity is an indulgence for the secure, street life precludes it.

In any case, small and basic pleasures are the most exquisite. He does not envy the harried lives of the affluent, sharp and bitter; their contentment is cosmetic. It can be wiped from them, easily.

Soft rain begins to fall. He collects up his briefcase and moves on. Across the great square and down into the Strand. The noise jars. Taxis and buses jostle, straggling revellers dodge between them. The lights are up at the Savoy as he passes. A glittering mannequin emerges, shimmering sequins and sable, spider legs, too many teeth, with a dark man in cashmere, claiming her.

Turning right he crosses the bridge and, dropping down, descends the steep staircase which takes him to the river's edge. The rain is falling steadily now, plummeting and swirling into the rushing water. Black and thick it has a heavy, greasy quality which would pull you down and hold you, hold you until all the breath has left you, only to spit you out at low tide.

He becomes aware of a presence next to him and, looking up, sees a policeman watching him. 'Evening.'

'Sir?' '

'Just watching the water, not thinking of throwing myself in, just watching.'

The policeman regards him. His lidded eyes are cold. 'The water, sir?' adding a note of sarcasm.

The steady beat of the rain becomes louder, filling all space. He can feel it dripping down his neck. His shoe is leaking. Picking up his briefcase, which he has leant on the wall, he makes as if to move away.

'Just one moment, sir.' A hint of malevolence. 'If I might, I would like to see what you have in there. Sir.' Emphasising the Sir, contemptuously.

The man holds it to him. 'You have no right . . .' he protests weakly, but what is the use. 'As you wish.' He opens it and offers the gaping mouth for inspection.

Bored, having made the kill, the policeman is not interested in the corpse. He gives the briefcase a cursory glance and waves it away.

'Then I'll wish you good night, Officer.' And he walks slowly and deliberately along the river wall.

Bastards, bloody bastards. The spell is broken, the night ruined. He longs for drink and company, has neither. North or south?

He turns north and walks steadily through the West End, past the rubicon of the Marylebone Road up into Primrose Hill. Entering the silent road that borders the hill he is relieved to see a light on at his destination. Elsie at least is predictable, and she always has booze.

He mounts the shabby worn steps of the once grand house and taps on the first floor window which abuts the door. The curtain opens and Elsie, wearing a grubby white turban, squints at him. Recognising him, she grins with delight and opens the window to hand him the key.

Cats are everywhere, mewing, clawing, purring. On the bed, on the floor, curled up on the bookcase, between the books, on the overmantle under the television, on it and beside it. On his entrance they curl and hiss and slither in irritation. The smell is overpowering, rank, acrid, lingering. Elsie sits, as usual, regal in her armchair. A tumbler of gin at her elbow, cigarette burning in the ashtray. Her cheeks are extravagantly rouged and glisten with sweat, it is very hot inside. Her eyes glitter. He's often wondered if she takes drugs. Her gaze is hard and bright.

Meanwhile the cats have scented the salami and fall upon the briefcase, tearing at the thin leather, mewing loudly. Bill kicks in their direction. They step back. One, a tabby, hisses softly. He swoops down, catches it by the tail and unceremoniously lobs it on to the bed. With the other hand he picks up the briefcase and finds the sandwich. Elsie takes it from him and, unpeeling the plastic cover, separates the bread from the fluorescent pink meat and feeds it to the cats weaving around her feet.

They have, both of them, seen better days. Their declining years are like the unravelling of a carefully knitted sweater that they have pieced together and that fate has caught like a nail and is now undoing. Slowly unwinding their dreams, their hopeful ambitions, soon all that will be left will be a pile of yarn, wrinkled and notched where the stitches had once been. A pile of wool all worn out and rumpled.

Elsie laughs. The booze is making her maudlin or is she coming down already? That last lot was deadly inferior, could they be ripping off such a sweet old lady? More than likely. Bill would be scandalised. Coke-sniffing granny of Primrose Hill. Ha! Ha! Life is rich, crazy.

Bill watches her muttering and laughing to herself. She's going off, dribbling her way into senility, he thinks. He shudders involuntarily and moves away, afraid of contagion.

'Have a drink, Bill, come on! You know you don't have to wait to be asked. Help yourself.'

Bill fills a tumbler with gin and, avoiding the feline swarms, turns on the radio. He is searching for dance tunes. Elsie and he have burnt some shoe leather on dance floors. She was a beautiful dancer. Wistful for those golden times he tunes the dial and finds what he is looking for.

He pulls Elsie to her feet and takes her in his practised arms. The cats, familiar with this hazard, melt into the walls and shadows. They watch critically.

Elsie and Bill spin effortlessly around the room, suddenly made larger and bolder. There is a faint impression of a glittering ball spinning on the ceiling, sending out silver rays dappling the carpet. The band, in white tuxedos, plays on.

Chapter Seven

☾

Candida lies in her bed listening to his rhythmic breathing, harmonising with the swishing of the cars as they drive through the rain. She is wide awake and restless. Frustrated, bored. Carefully sliding from the bed she pulls on her kimono and tiptoes out, closing the door behind her. The fire is still glowing. She rakes the embers listlessly. Once, long ago, she had seen salamanders in the fire. She had been tripping and had watched them the whole night, weaving and dancing. No salamanders now. She is drained, exhausted. Men had a way of sucking all the life force from her, while at the same time she grew larger and larger, piling on pounds as if frantically trying to fill the void.

A man she once knew practised tantra, he told her he drew energy from women as he made love to them. Like a kind of vampire; he sucked his women dry. They had been lovers, but hearing this drunken boast she threw him out. She knew he was right but also how she colluded with the theft, countering it took too much energy.

All she can do is endure the bloke until he leaves. Which he would, sooner rather than later. When the weather improved. She looks at her table. The cards are still there, dusty. There have been no clients for a while; he keeps them away. Her energy is low and inward, people are not drawn to her. She looks at the last spread, the Hanged Man, Death, Temperance.

She feels like the Hanged Man, suspended like a chrysalis on a leaf. Waiting. Inert, upended, helpless. The figure like a god has a halo around his inverted head and he beams at her from the secret life of the card. What he beams escapes her. She is not enlightened, but weighed down, stuffed, like a sofa. She drags herself through the day, waiting for release. She knows these times presage change but, like the eighth month of pregnancy, waiting is all that can be done. Enduring, bearing the weight, marking time.

Panther has all but disappeared. He blends in with the background to such a degree that sometimes she cannot find him at all. He is sulky, petulant and swishes his tail a great deal. She watches the rain listlessly, the light of the street lamp shows the relentless heavy downpour. She wants to be out, out in the street, inside doesn't interest her now, it is contaminated.

Emerging from a corner the panther stands beside her. They exchange glances. She takes hold of a pile of discarded clothes and pulls them on. Finding her key and bag they stealthily let themselves out of the house. On the porch they breathe the cold night. They both seem to swell and shrink, to become more solid. As though the atoms of the night diffuse into them and transform them. They fly down the steps into the slashing rain, round the corner and are gone.

Crossing the road under the railway bridge they pass through the deserted market. The wooden stalls are chained together. Red and green wooden wheels and planked tops with the names of their owners carved in copperplate script. They seem forlorn, redundant, but also timeless. They will outlive the barrowboys who drag them out on early mornings.

Unusually they take the curved park road. The rain is easing and the stillness of late, late, night fills the air. A light is on in one of the large bay windows, they see two shadows moving. As they draw closer she realises they are dancing, faintly she hears band music as two blurs dance gently around the room.

They go up on to the hill. A crescent moon is just emerging, slipping in and out of the cloud. Venus twinkles close by. Climbing the rise the hawthorns leap and twist in the shadows. Murmuring, the wind crackles the branches of the oak trees. To her right and far off glows the red light of the West End. Babylon, its tentacles glistening in the night mists.

She stands and stretches and takes a lungful of air, shakes her hair from its plait. A low mist is curling up the hill and collecting in pockets around the bushes and the squat trees. The grass underfoot is still with frost, it crunches pleasantly as she walks on it. Her feet leave dark footsteps splayed behind her. There is silence, just the faint electrical hum of the city. She looks down and sees a million flickering lights, recognises the Tower, behind the skyscrapers of the city, and the dome of St Paul's. Low cloud clings to the tops of the highest buildings, she hears the far away drone of an airplane and can faintly make out the red glow of a tail light. Looking with unfocused eyes the city glitters like a far-off treasure.

Gazing at the lights she fails to notice a figure looming out of the darkness. Cat hisses loudly and she turns alarmed, angry to be caught so unawares. It is a very large man, six foot or more and strongly built. Her heart misses a beat and she instinctively protects herself. He stops some distance from her.

'It's all right, I didn't mean to startle you.' He stands and waits.

'I was lost in thought.'

'The city; so seductive it draws you in but drags you down. Dangerous, beautiful but dangerous.'

The moon slides out and she catches a glimpse of his face. Light-coloured hair, beard. He looks like a Viking or an East Coast Celt. He doesn't feel dangerous. Automatically she looks down at the panther. He is watching him carefully too, but seems unalarmed, tail down he stands neutral pose.

'This hill is an old hill.'

'The Druids come here.'

He laughs. 'Yes, the Druids come here, straight from their offices and banks. Ha! Ha! The Druids come here!'

'And the gay boys, they come here too.'

'Are you a Druid then?'

'Me, no, not a Druid. A diviner perhaps, but not an anything. And you? What are you?'

'I'm the Lord of Misrule.' He laughs. 'Yes, I'm the Lord of Misrule, and you, you must be the Lady of Camellias. Ha! Ha!' She feels offended. He is laughing at her.

'Well, I'll be off then,' she says and turns away and begins walking down the hill.

'Don't go! Oh, come on, I was only joking! Come on! Come and have a drink with me!'

She pauses. There is something interesting about him. What is he doing on the Hill, her hill? She is sure she has not seen him before. Perhaps he is a ghost, an axe murderer, or worse still, a poet.

'Okay, but where? Camden's dead this time of night.'

'My bus is just around the corner. Come!'

He offers her his arm, she takes it bemused, coolly, and they walk down Primrose Hill together.

The bus is a bus. She had expected a camper van or ex-GPO van or VW Bus but it was a lifesize LT Routemaster, double decker. Painted blue with curtains at the windows. It is parked in a side road. The bus is glorious in its great bulk. So much, so big, so blue.

'Welcome to my kingdom!'

He shows her inside.

Most of the seats had been removed except for the long benches by the door. Instead a gallery kitchen had been fitted, tiny stove, fridge and sink.

'But it's beautiful!' Tiny cupboards painted marigold hang overhead, and a small table, tomato red with two chairs also blue sits down with it. The cat jumps on one of the long seats and curls up. Dried sage and lavender hang in bunches, next to onion strings and garlic. There is even a pot of winter jasmine. He lights the gas and puts the kettle on.

'Sit down, sit down! Take your coat off. Roll a joint.'

He throws a leather pouch on to the table and lights a yellow candle which gives off a sweet beeswax smell. She slides off her cape and busies herself with the grass. What bliss it is to be the one receiving. It strikes her how long it has been since someone has bustled around her with cups of tea and sympathy. A tear winkles its way down her cheek, and then another, until she finds herself sobbing, her forehead resting on the table.

He turns around astonished, then smiling draws his chair

alongside and lays his cheek beside hers. She becomes aware of his warm solid presence and cries more ferociously until she is howling with anguish. The incongruity of their position strikes them simultaneously and they break into helpless giggles, then more tears, then giggles, until exhausted they notice the bus has filled with steam.

'Shit! The kettle!' He jumps up and turns off the gas. Not a drop is left. It is red hot.

'You're a bad influence on me. I almost burnt my lovely kettle.' He smiles, but there is an edge to his voice. He fills the kettle again and sets it on the gas; it hisses and steams, red hot.

'I suppose you've cried all over the grass as well.' Which she has, but it is not beyond repair.

'Move over, let me do this!' he pushes her gently. Electric shocks between them. She doesn't budge an inch but enjoys him pushing her.

He is big, much much bigger than she is, which makes her feel relaxed. His hair is shoulder length and red gold in colour, it is thick and curled at the ends. He looks leonine, glorious. His skin has the freshness of a country dweller. It has a faint ruddy tan. His eyes are large and greenish brown. He has a long moustache which droops into a thick beard. He really is a Saxon, one of the big boned, fair, booming warriors. She sees him standing majestic in a long boat . . . 'Who are you?' she asks.

'I'm Uther Pendragon.'

Despite herself she lets out a loud cackle.

He turns to her slowly, she has to admit majestically. 'King of the Britons.' She looks at him trying not to laugh, tears running down her face, biting her lip desperately. She fails and collapses for a second time on his table.

She raises her head gingerly, 'God, what a sight!'

Without a mirror but with some imagination she has to agree. Wet hair stuck to her cheeks, her mascara has run and is now wiped on to the backs of her hands. A mess.

'I'm sorry it was so rude of me to laugh. I expect everyone does . . .' she trails off, realising this only made things worse.

The tea is hot and sweet, a cinnamon mixture. He produces cake, poppy seed. It appears home-made, she wonders aloud where the woman is who made it.

He lies, 'My mother, actually.' Their eyes meet.

Quickly she changes the subject.

'You can see the cat, can't you? I knew you were, er, um ...'

'A little strange?'

'Well, yes, that's one way of putting it. But not really. It's the others, those who can't see who are crazy, sick, lost.'

'So the mad ones are normal and the normals are crazy?'

'Yes, but because they are crazy they will go to any lengths to hide the fact. They lock up the sane ones – anyone who is in the wrong place at the wrong time – and make sure they never get a chance to say what they know. Like the witches ...'

'Don't talk about witches! It's bad luck!'

'See, you believe it too. The lie.'

'Look, it's dangerous! I know. I know someone who lost her job, because they found out she read the cards ... she was a teacher. Said she was a corrupting influence. She thought they were joking, didn't take them seriously. She lost her job ... she loved it ... the kids ... she went kind of crazy afterwards ... quietly ... sat at home and cried looking at the wall ... To her it was only a game, she didn't understand how seriously they took it. They were Christians ... you know ... the hanging and flogging kind.'

'They said I was crazy ...'

'Yea.'

'Because I wouldn't speak. I just looked at them. They tried everything ... Then they gave up ... I was lucky. No one sent me to the bin ... In the end they just ignored me ... They left me alone. Girls I knew went crazy ... Got locked up ... Slashed their wrists ... Overdosed.'

'Jesus, where'd you grow up? Broadmoor?'

'No, the Home Counties ... it's worse there, schizoid people. schizoid life.' She shudders. 'I got out, as soon as I could.'

She reaches her hand across to his and holds it. Gratefully, peacefully she leans against his soft woollen bulk. She smells sandalwood and woodsmoke and man. He reaches his arm around her and she puts her head on his shoulder. He kisses her gently on the forehead. They sit quietly listening to the rustling of the trees.

He leans over and kisses her softly on the mouth, on her closed eyelids, then her mouth again rougher.

'Come upstairs.'

'But . . .'

'Come on.'

She follows him up the narrow stairs.

Chapter Eight

The taxi speeds through the darkened streets. The rain has stopped, the tyres splash on the wet road. They sit in silence. The boy and the man. The man holds the boy's hand as if afraid he might jump out of the cab. He can't, the doors are locked. The boy is sweating heavily but he is not hot. He is afraid. The man's hand is dry, cool like paper. He has long, slim fingers which are carefully manicured and a gold signet ring. Tasteful and discreet.

The boy notices the locked doors at the moment he thinks of bolting. He sits back sulkily. His heart echoes like a lonely bell in his chest, his ears sing with chorusing flies. The buzzing is almost unbearable. His mouth dry, he looks helplessly at the man's patrician profile. He wishes, oh he wishes, so many things. A bed, a room, a friend. He wishes he were not here, but where else might he be? He has no one and nothing. Is there another place? Death, maybe death. Sensing his gaze the face turns and softens slightly as their eyes meet.

'Nearly there,' he says and squeezes his hand.

The taxi bowls up Portland Place passing the huge stucco buildings, the Embassies, mansion blocks. The wide street is deserted, flash cars bumper to bumper by the roadside. Wealth and privilege ooze from their gleaming coachwork. Turning into the Nash terrace they are thrown together. The man's body does not yield but the boy feels him tremble.

They stop at the lights and right themselves, each looking away. He feels a trickle of sweat working its way down his chest. He aches to take his clothes off and stand under running water. To wash off the grime, the woodsmoke, the filth of the tunnels. But nothing will wash off the dirt inside. No soap, no disinfectant can kill the flies which breed and breed and one day . . . It is that which scares him. One day their buzzing might make him do something awful. He'd killed the dog. He'd killed the dog and enjoyed it. Only afterwards had he felt a sick pain in his belly.

They cross into the park. It grows darker. Just past the turning to the Inner Circle the cab draws up. The doors are unlocked and they get out. The man pays the cabby and, taking firm hold of his elbow, propels the boy into the darkened street.

He is shaken from his trance, he'd expected a flat, a shower a bed with clean sheets. Terror grips him. He watches the cab disappear into the night.

'Hey! Where are you taking me? Hey!' The boy tries to wrestle his arm free but finds it twisted far up his back. He tries kicking but the man, who hadn't seemed so substantial, holds him tight. He pushes him forwards. The boy stumbles and finds another arm across his throat.

'One word out of you and you've had it? Understand.' The man speaks in his ear. His voice is thick with contempt, fury. 'Trash like you doesn't deserve to live. Now shut up and get moving.'

There is a hole in the hedge. Pushing the boy down and forwards, together they squeeze through into the park. The darkness is a shock. Only faintly can he distinguish the outline of trees. Time slows as he allows himself to be pulled across the sodden grass. He clicks into another self. His will becomes limp, his body empty and numb. All he wants is oblivion.

Walking on the path now, they make their way down the incline. A figure appears out of the darkness and without speaking takes his free arm. To his astonishment it is a woman's hand.

'It's okay,' she says. 'You won't get hurt if you don't struggle.' Her voice sounds soft but there is a deathlike quality to it. Like the slaughterer before he slits the throat. Calming the dumb beast.

Terror is cold and damp. It lodges heavily in his gut. His mouth is parched, he tries to swallow but can't. His ears buzz as he strains to see where he is. He dares not turn and look at them. But glimpsing sideways sees a blur of skirt, hears the soft footfall of brogues.

They reach the edge of a lake fenced off by high iron railings. There is a hut. Several people are milling around in the darkness, it is hard to make anything out in the gloom. The water glitters. He realises the moon has come out. It slips from behind some clouds and the tiny waves become silver tipped. It is cold. A damp breeze chills him.

As they draw near the talking stops.

He is pushed forwards and they group around him. He spins around and around. Like a trapped animal, half-crouching he wishes he had his knife. But it is lost. The flies, silenced by shock, awake in a frenzy. They buzz and hum and beat their frenzied wings against his head. They stream out of his mouth and ears. Flailing he strikes out and tries to beat a way through the bodies. They move in closer. He smells alcohol fumes. He tries to scream but no sound comes. Someone pulls at his coat. It rips. Laughter. Another hand, or the same one, pulls at his trousers, the waistband gives. He feels them slide over his hips. Holding them up he is defenceless, hands grab at him from all directions.

They are laughing, tearing his clothes and laughing. He begins to cry, huge sobs catch behind his teeth. Despair floods over him. He falls forward on to the soft grass. It is sodden and churned by their feet but the smell of dirt and the grit consoles him. Later, he remembers hoping he hadn't fallen in any dog shit. They crowd over him. Someone sits astride him. One by one they take turns.

His mouth open, he finds pieces of earth, grit, grass, mixed up with his tongue and teeth. He tastes blood and idly wonders what is bleeding, apart from his ass. Just before he loses consciousness he realises the flies are silent. He wonders if that means he is dead.

Chapter Nine

In the armchair Bill snores softly. His long limbs lie awkwardly on the worn carpet. His head has fallen back and to the side, leaving his mouth open and whistling with each snore. Elsie watches him tenderly, her bed a sea of cats, asleep as dawn approaches. Faint stirrings can be heard in the trees outside. But no sleep for Elsie. She is as perky as ever. The coke was not so bad after all. Probably cut with speed. Her body hums in a jagged way.

This is the best time. Exhausted peace of night, expectant silence of dawn. She sits in her bed stroking her cats. Purring, twitching cat-flesh. The ginger tom is having a catty dream, his little paws run jerkily along the pink candlewick.

She hasn't troubled to undress but put her nightie on top of her day clothes; the cotton neck ruffle looks incongruous over amber beads. Her white hair is nicely permed but she has left off the turban: it was too hot for dancing in.

Bastards. They didn't know who they tangled with. Thought she was just a little old lady. Lost fifty quid she had, off to score a line and had taken a short cut through the market. Old, she was an easy target. Even though she didn't carry a handbag, hadn't for years.

Still, money is easy to come by these days. Things have been on the up and up since she'd met that bloke. Something vaguely troubles her about him. A cold fish. Nice of him to find homes for all those kids, though. Poor babies sleeping in shop doorways, rumpled in blankets, grey-faced, shivering with the cold. But she isn't sure where this hostel is. There's something not quite right about the set up.

But the money is good. It helps with the little habit she is developing. She'd had a pipe for years. But the Chinaman had died and the new lot didn't want outsiders around. The door had shut in her face. She first thought that after a lifetime of dope she should give it all a rest and stick to tea and digestives. But habits die hard. The old pains returned. There wasn't much now. Her looks had gone, together with the gentlemen, but the aching stayed the same. The little smoke gave her good dreams, dulled the edges. She'd missed it.

One day she had bumped into one of the boys upstairs, a funny looking bunch. Dead skinny, all in black, skulls and daggers, dyed black hair. Hammer Horrors she'd called them. Wet behind the ears though, a bunch of middle-class kids slumming. Nice enough to her. Respectful. One day she'd bumped into one of them, aching for a smoke she was, and asked him. He looked pale enough, grey rings under his eyes, like the old Chinaman's friends. She'd braved it and asked him if he could get some.

He had stopped dead in his tracks and turned round to face her.

'You know, a smoke.'

'You smoke! Jesus!' She could tell he was impressed.

'The man I used to get it off . . .' she fudged.'

'You're serious! My God! . . . Come upstairs, I'll give you some.'

'Bring it down, will you? My legs aren't so good.'

He'd brought some weed, which wasn't what she'd had in mind at all. Not strong enough. She looked at it, her disappointment evident.

'No, I meant . . . opium.'

'Bloody hell, no one smokes that stuff anymore. Do they?'

'Well . . .'

'What about Chinatown?' He looked at her and thought about the problems seeking out a dealer might bring, if you were seventy-odd and a bit wobbly on your legs.

'Well, I've got some coke. Ever tried that?' He wondered if her heart could stand it.

'Coke?'

'Yea, coke, you sniff it, makes you happy.'

'Sniff it?'

Which is how it had all started. Nice but pricey. But she saved on food, only wanting tea and fags. Soon enough, she needed other ways to get money. Then she'd bumped into this geezer. He was talking to one of the doorstep kids, she'd noticed, and wondered what he was up to. Bloke in a suit. Upper class. Nice brogues, handmade. Next day kid was gone. She only remembered this a few days later when she saw the same bloke talking to another kid. She waited until he'd gone and asked the girl what he was up to.

'Dunno, some kind of social worker.'

'Social worker? In those clothes?'

'Asked me if I wanned to go to a hostel. But I did'na.'

'A hostel? Where?'

'Dunno, did'na say. Spare some change?'

She gave her 10p. Walking off she hadn't noticed that the man had stopped to watch their conversation. She almost bumped into him.

'Excuse me. I couldn't help overhearing . . .' Cut-glass accent. He leant over her. She flustered, then composed herself.

'I saw you talking to the lad who used to sleep there.'

'Yes, luckily we managed to find him a place . . .'

'A place?'

'Yes, it's so difficult . . . but we were lucky with him.'

'A place? Where exactly?' Her voice hardened. There was something shifty, vague about him.

'We're a charity, for the homeless . . . I'm voluntary, of course . . .'

'Of course.'

'But we do what we can.'

'Ah.'

'Well, I must be getting on . . .' He lifted his hat and turned away.

She realised he had yet to tell her where the hostel was. But stayed silent as he walked away. She smelt a rat. 'Wait. Wait!'

He stopped.

'Perhaps I can help you?'

He turned. Smiling wanly, 'What sort of help did you have in mind?'

'Well . . . I need a bit of extra, on top of my pension, maybe there's some office work, or I can talk to the kids. They know me. They trust me, you see. Not much, just to make things a bit easier . . . you know.'

She looked him straight in the eye.

They gazed a brief second.

'Shall we discuss it over a glass?'

They had crossed the road and gone into the busy pub. Elsie found a table toward the back of the room and watched him as he walked to the bar. He bought her a gin. The barman raised his eyebrows when he saw her company. She winked.

'What charity exactly?'

'Let me give you my card.' He looked unsuccessfully through his pockets. 'I am sorry, don't seem to have one on me.'

'Pity.'

'But to your kind offer . . . I'm sure we can work something out. Haven't I seen you somewhere? Your face seems familiar . . .' A sly look passed across his face. 'Soho perhaps?'

She smiled. They were beginning to understand one another. 'It's possible . . . go there much do you? I wouldn't have thought you were one for the girls . . .?'

He returned a stony look. She took a sip of gin. Was he dangerous? Could be . . . go easy.

'. . . but if there is anything I can do to help you?'

'Yes, yes.' He seemed distracted now. Maybe she'd gone too far. . .

Silence.

She waited.

He was thinking.

'Perhaps I could telephone you . . . when there is a vacancy? . . . We would of course pay you for your trouble.'

'Boys, I take it . . .'

'Yes we work mainly with . . . young boys.'

Of course she knew, they knew, the boys that is, but most of them had not much else going for them. Besides she'd done it herself, when her legs went and she couldn't dance any more. Not much, none of your street work, discreet to pay the bills, buy a little smoke or a nice hat. She was partial to hats. Finding them was easy, they hung around the tube, outside certain clubs. She had a friend, Mickey, who'd explain the score and bring them to her place, he got a cut, not much, to pay for his habit.

He called every two weeks or so. Came in a cab. Always paid cash. She made the boys wash, gave them a meal and sent them off. The funny thing was she never saw them again. Guessed he paid well enough to set them on their feet. She didn't believe this either. But didn't dwell on it. Sink or swim. They were all in the same leaking boat. People like him were okay but the rest of us . . . fighting for their leavings.

Bill snores himself awake and looks dopily around trying to work out where he is. Elsie has drifted off, propped up against her pillows. He thinks resentfully of her soft warm bed. She won't let him share it. Never had. He doesn't know why. But his aching bones could do with it right now. He tries unsuccessfully to rearrange himself but he is too uncomfortable. Miserably he looks at the grey light of morning. He is too old for this caper. The catty smell is overpowering and his mouth has a sour taste from the cheap gin. He shivers and wonders if he dares hop into bed with her, but decides not.

Breakfast. He'll walk across the park. There's a caff off Titchfield, round the back. He'll have breakfast, then a bet. He is a bit low. Instinctively he looks round for her bag. It is open. Has she left it there on purpose? She gives him little handouts sometimes. It is stuffed with money. He is surprised, he knows she has some racket going. He slips a twenty out and puts on his coat.

Elsie watches him through her eyelashes and tries to hold the smile. The predictability of his actions is reassuring. He is a dear old thing.

'Oh, are you going, Bill?' She feigns sleep.

'Yes, old girl, the chair's too hard. You won't let me have the bed.'

'Best this way. You okay for money?'

'Well.' He shifts his feet.

'Take a twenty, there's one in my bag.' Wicked, but why not?

'Er, thanks.' He bends over the bag and rustles the contents, pretending to slip a note in his trousers. He looks at her sheepishly and walks over to the bed to kiss her on the cheek.

'See you. Thanks.'

'Take care, love.'

He closes the door quietly. She hears him pause at the top of the stone steps before he treads heavily down them and into the street.

Chapter Ten

He wakes up alone. Where is the bitch? Her side is unslept in. He slides out and pulls on his clothes. He is hungry; he is cold. Where is the bloody fat cow? In the living room there are a few embers; he pokes them but there is no coal. 'Damn!'

She is not here. He goes into the kitchen and fills the kettle. Plugging it in he scans the kitchen. Painted green and red. What kind of colour is that! Looks like a squat. Plants and papers stacked with jars of weird looking food. All brown and hard. Windows are cloudy and dirty plates and cups are spread around the sink.

'Useless! Bloody useless!'

He opens the fridge, takes out some eggs, butter and milk. But when he looks for bread there is none. 'Shit!'

The kettle boils and switches itself off. He opens the cupboard and looks for the coffee, nope, but finds the tea, He washes out a cup, carefully rinsing it in boiling water from the kettle.

He takes it to the table, a rickety wooden one and sits down. A pile of unopened letters is next to some twine, a little plant with dusty leaves, a pair of black sequinned gloves, a black hat, some loose change. He looks through the pile of letters. No cheques, a red bill. Some pencils. Junk! Junk for a junk life.

He gulps a mouthful of tea. It is bitter, he spits it out in the sink. No bloody sugar either! But he finds the bowl on the tabletop. It is brown. He stirs in three spoonfuls. It makes the tea taste funny. But here he is on funny farm, so what does he expect?

Time to move on. He is tired of the baggage, she is fed up with him too, but is waiting for him to make the move. When he is ready. Needs a bit more time to pull this one off. A bloke knows someone who wants a driver. To bring in some hot videos from Amsterdam. He is waiting for the word and he'll be off. He has a deal of his own he'll do there. Kill two birds at once. Just has to wait it out with the fat cow then he'll be off. Bye, bye.

A weak chorus of birdsong breaks out. He stands up and stretches. A run, that's what he'll do. Nice long run in the park to get the old adrenaline moving. He finds his running gear and changes, pausing to check his body out. Not bad, not bad, slim but all muscle, no fat on him. He pulls on his hooded sweatshirt and sits down to tie up his running shoes. They are wearing thin on the outside; he runs light but uneven. They'll do until he's done the trip, then he'll buy some really neat ones.

He closes the door behind him and sniffs the air. It is drizzling slowly, grey, misty, cold. He puts the hood up and jogs briskly down the street. Once he catches the rhythm of the running, his mind unravels and stretches. He loses himself observing the streets. Under the railway arch, through the market, he'll go over the Hill and down into Regent's, which will be open by now. The drizzle turns to rain and he moves into long-distance gear, head down, movements kept to a minimum.

He allows his mind to wander. Amazing what comes up. Old memories, people float in front of him. He crosses the road on to Primrose Hill and, running steadily, takes the hill, up and along and then down towards the road. No traffic. He crosses and runs past the zoo buildings across the narrow bridge over the canal. He avoids a dog walker, their eyes sliding past one another. A faint patch of sunlight breaks through the clouds.

Across the Outer Circle and into the park. He leaves the path and runs alongside the perimeter hedges. The grass is sodden, heavy with several days' rain. A low mist is rising in the distance. A little sweat is building, he sinks his breathing further into his chest. His legs tirelessly pound the soft grass. It is harder in the wet but good for building muscle. He looks at his legs as they move rhythmically. He loves his body. The only reliable thing. Tuned like a fine motor.

He is in control. It obeys.

He runs around the outside of the tennis courts and along the hedges. Crows are waddling in the long grass, caw-cawing they watch him but do not fly off. Cocky birds these crows. All the animals in the park are people trained. They move with slow disdain out of the path of children, footballs, tourists. Grey squirrels are sitting on their haunches watching and burrowing in the soft earth.

The sky is leaden grey, heavy and dull. The air mists as he exhales. There are no leaves on the trees, it is the dead time before spring. Everything seems tired out, hard, rigid, as though the effort of surviving winter has drained the lifeforce. People, plants, animals are wilting, aching for warmth, light, hope.

But he likes this time. The barrenness suits his lean hard world. There are no frills, no soft edges. Tarmac, concrete, ugliness, ignorance, poverty. He knows it, likes it; feels at home with the wastelands, boarded up houses, dole queues. He won't be a mug like the rest, getting saddled with a wife and bawling kids, a council house and beer gut. Not likely. He'll get out. Somewhere warm, Marbella maybe. The good life. Just needs a couple of good deals and he'll be off.

Behind him he can hear animal shrieks from the zoo, elephants or something. The ground is getting boggier as it slopes down toward the lake. In front and to the right the huge bronzed dome of the mosque glowing dully in the morning light. The traffic is starting up, driving into the West End. A few birds sing listlessly. A dog gambols across the grass; he stiffens ready to kick out. Dogs sometimes attack, you can never be sure. This one veers off when its owner, a big blond bloke, calls him away.

He sees the boating lake draw closer; he is breathing hard, the damp always makes him wheeze. He'll like living in the sun, it will help his chest. But today, no sun; it is going to be a grey day. He takes the path around the lake, he is beginning to feel tired, he decides to take the Inner Circle. He turns to his left, slowing down as he runs on to the path.

Past the children's playground, swings and slides. The boating pool is drained, small boats are chained together at one end. Large brown and white Canada geese waddle on the grass with a few seagulls. He crosses the bridge and glances over, some black swans are gliding gently away. Other birds he does not recognise bob on the water. He turns to the right by the boating hut and stops dead in his tracks. A leg, unclothed and at a strange angle is sticking out from the shrubbery. An old man is bending over what looks like a body. Hearing him approach, the old man looks up, ashen-faced. The bloke wobbles and skids to a halt beside them. The old man grabs his arm.

'Help me! Help me! Something awful has happened.'

Chapter Eleven

☾

They wake together, neither has slept well, unaccustomed to each other's sounds and body movements. He leans over her and kisses her nose. She smiles sleepily: he was okay, this one, slow, careful, very sensual; she could do with more a lot more of this. She pulls him over her and they make love again, quicker this time, is he in a hurry?

He watches her beneath him, cool, pleased with himself. She is warm and luxurious, so different from skinny Jane, an embarrassment of flesh. He wonders how he can have both, if he could keep it up. He smiles, she smiles back, he smiles more. They sleep fitfully afterwards; he is thinking of Jane, wishing she was there to cook his breakfast. He guesses that etiquette demands he get up and make it. He doesn't want to, neither does he want her nosing about the bus; this thought makes him open his eyes. No, must get her out now!

'Are you awake?'

She murmurs dozing.

He shakes her. 'Day's wasting . . .'

She pulls herself up and looks around as if trying to remember the night before. Uther swings on top of her to block her vision. 'Let's get up.'

She peers out through the net curtains. 'It's daylight already.'

'Yea, but I don't feel sleepy. I'm stiff though.'

She stands up and arches her back.

'And hungry . . .'

'Let's go and get breakfast somewhere.'

'But where?'

'Let's walk across the park and find a caff on the other side.'

They dress quickly, the bus is freezing. Candida notices a pair of knickers, pink cotton protruding from under the bed. She looks around and sees signs of a woman, discreet but obvious. She remembers the home-made cake.

'Live here alone?'

'Yea,' he lies badly, they both know it. Candida looks away in contempt. Humiliated, she'd thought it was another thing, but it wasn't, only the same thing, another one-off. She says nothing. Acid burns in her stomach, she grinds her teeth and smiles grimly through them. Uther is humming a tune, oblivious.

Downstairs they dress up with scarves, hats, jumpers and leave the fuggy damp air of the bus. Outside the grey light of dawn stings their eyes. Candida wears a soft black velvet hat. Her red hair shines in contrast. It is unbound and flutters gently as they walk towards the hill.

'You have beautiful hair. It's so long. Such an amazing colour.'

'I can sit on it. I love my hair, it's the bit of me I like best. I feel like a mermaid combing it and sitting on a rock.'

'Luring men to their doom?' It is a joke.

'No, it's the other way round. They trap me and suck me dry.' She spits this out, venomous. For the first time she remembers the man she left sleeping in her bed. Should she say something? No, best not.

'Men? No way. We spend our time avoiding you lot and your rampant hormones!'

'What?!'

'Especially once you get to thirty. Hungry-eyed women looking for sperm, with house-trained, sexy, well-off, obedient owners. Ha! Ha! It's you lot who're the vampires. Don't think we don't know it, either. Women think men are so thick. We know what you all want, even if you've got padded shoulders and briefcases.' Post coital hatred seeps out of him.

'And what might that be?' she asks heatedly.

'A cottage with roses around the door, two beautiful children and a rich, sexy bloke to bring home the bacon.'

'It's not what I want!' she lies.

'Liar!'

'Look, it's men who're the vampires. As soon as you let them into your bed they suck you dry. They never have money, bum off you, don't clear up or cook or shop. When they meet you they say they like you the way you are and then they set about criticising the way you do things and putting you down. When they've taken all they can they dump you for a younger, more compliant, model.'

They are shouting, standing in the middle of the road. Both have red faces and mists of steam come from their mouths. A milk float glides past. The driver leans out and grins at Uther.

'And you all gang up together and tell filthy jokes while you beat and kill us!'

'A woman never hit a man I suppose! Don't give me that crap!'

'Even if I did I wouldn't kill you. Worst luck!'

'Hey! Hey! Who's talking about killing? Come on.'

'That's right. *You* start the argument and when *you* begin to lose you start saying what's all the fuss about.'

'Listen!'

'Listen nothing. Shit! *You make me sick*!' She screeches so loudly a window is raised in the road.

'Bloody shut up. You stupid bitch!' It slams shut.

'See! He agrees with me!'

'*Piss off*!' She storms off across the road. A cyclist wobbles dangerously as she passes him.

Stunned, he stands looking as she climbs the hill.

She puffs to the top of the hill. She wants more than anything to turn round but she will not. Sod him! Who needs the bloody bastards when it comes down to it. And another thing! That parasite in her bed was going to get out too. Enough of this crap. Out he would go. *Today*!

She turns around and walks down the hill. She'll go home this instant and chuck the bugger out. She strides out of the park and crosses the road. She feels a pang as she passes the bus but thrusts her chin forwards and marches off. The curtains are drawn in any case. He's probably gone to sleep. She'll see him later. Now, she has a mission.

Storming down the road she passes the grinning milkman and gives him the cold eye. Her whole body bounces and vibrates as she stomps along the pavement. The panther streams alongside, ears flat, tail taut but low.

In the market the boys are dragging the barrows out. Cardboard boxes of fruit are piled on the pavement. Bananas, mangoes, Spanish oranges. Flowers mass in large metal vases, gladioli, irises, bunches of budded tulips, red and yellow, carmine, magnolia.

''Allo darling, wot's yer hurry?'

'Piss off!'

'Sorry,' he mimics back in a high Widow-Twankey voice.

'Fat cow!' jeers another, his nine-month beer belly flops over his trousers. Piggy eyes, bulbous red nose.

She closes her eyes, trying to keep her mouth shut. These battles get nasty quickly. Head down she walks out onto the High Street. The wall of hostility is palpable. Sometimes, just sometimes she wishes she is six foot three and twenty stone, then she'd have a bloody argument.

Under the railway bridge, past the shops. She reaches her door just as a taxi is drawing up. Funny. The door opens and the bloke gets out, dressed in running gear, splattered with mud. Then a bundle, a person, is carried out, wrapped in a thick brown overcoat. He looks unconscious, drunk. Finally an old man, in a jumper and shirt emerges. The man from the tunnels!

What the hell? They pay the driver and stand holding the bundle who is wobbling dangerously. His legs buckle and the bloke picks him up and throws him over his shoulder. The three of them unsteadily make their way up the stone steps.

'What's going on?' She runs up to them.

'Open the bloody door will you! He's heavy.'

Obediently she opens it. 'Is he drunk?'

'No!'

'Hurt?'

'Yea.'

'I thought he was dead.' The older man spoke.

They walk slowly up the stairs. For a selfish bastard he is carrying the boy with exquisite tenderness.

She opens the door to the flat.

'Where?'

'In my bed, no, put him by the fire; he's freezing and needs warming up.'

He lays him tenderly down. The boy groans in agony.

'On his front! Turn him over.'

They find a cushion for his head and turn him slowly. They crouch around him. He looks awful. Grey-faced, blood-streaked, mud around his mouth. His eyes are half-open.

'You think we should call an ambulance? He looks really bad. He might die.'

'Or the police?'

The two men look incredulous.

'Don't be daft!'

'What happened?'

'Wait, make a cup of tea and we'll sit down and talk. I don't feel so good.' The old man did look ashen, drained.

She makes a big pot, extra strong, and seeing half a bottle of whisky puts that on the tray too. When she comes into the room both men are sitting by the boy, but looking away from him and each other. They look up as she put the tray down.

'At last!'

'Put some whisky in, it'll warm you up.'

'Good idea.' The bloke looks at her and smiles; her motherly bustling is reassuring. He feels almost warm towards her.

'Here, drink this,' She hands a mug to Bill. 'Tea topped up with scotch.'

'Thanks.'

They drink their tea almost as if they have forgotten the boy. He lies still. They can hear his rough breathing.

'Well . . . ?'

'We found him in the park . . .'

'Well, I found him . . . haven't I seen you . . .'

'Yes, you're the man from the tunnels.'

'Oh, yes. He's the boy with the dog . . .'

'Is he?' She leans forwards. She didn't remember his face, just the blood.

'Oh God, that poor dog . . .' She feels sick remembering.

'But what happened? Has he been attacked?'

'I don't know, I found him lying in the bushes in the park.'

'I was running and nearly bumped into him. Gave me the shock of my life.'

He fails to mention how he'd tried to run on and Bill had stopped him. Threatened him and made him carry the body to the road. Didn't mention how he'd thrown up when Bill explained what he thought had happened. How he'd argued with him to call an ambulance and be done with it. How Bill, who'd he'd seen around with some hard men, had reminded him that favours always had a way of being repaid. They'd covered him in Bill's coat and got the poor bastard to his feet. He was moaning but alive. Slowly they'd walked to the road. An old bag walking her pooch had said, 'How disgusting!' She thought he was drunk and hoped the cabbie would think the same. A suspicious bunch cabbies, always worried about riff raff in their cabs. Noise, dirt, fags, vomit. Still Bill had found one, someone he knew. Seemed to know bloody everyone this geezer did. It crossed the bloke's mind that this favour might do him well. And they'd bundled him in the cab. The boy was moaning. Bill leant over and told him to shut it or they'd be walking. He shut up.

'But what happened?'

Bill looks at the bloke and he looks straight back.

'Looks like he got well and truly buggered.'

'Oh God!'

'Was on the game though. Wasn't he?'

'What bloody difference does that make?'

'Well . . . I only thought.'

Bill looks at him coldly.

'Poor bastard.'

'What's his name?'

'No idea.'

The boy who is listening to all of this keeps his eyes closed. He recognises Bill's voice and is softly grateful that it was he who found him. Bill has been kind to him before, brought him food, tea, sometimes. A tear slips, and falls down his cheek. It stings where the flesh has been grazed.

'Would you like some tea?' Candida leans forward. 'Can you hear me?'

He opens his eyes. A large head with red hair, leaning down smiling at him. He nods.

She pushes a mug of tea towards him; it smells of whisky. He slowly turns on to one side and leans up on his elbow. Everything hurts. Everything. It is too much effort, he sinks down again, and drifts off. Someone covers him with a duvet and the warmth of the fire slowly unfreezes his body. He fades as they talk softly, somewhere, far away.

'I'll come back this afternoon. I want to ask around . . . find the bastards who did this.'

'Oh, what's the point. It could have been anyone, faggots or queer bashers, the police even. Anyone . . . I'd leave well alone.'

'I'm not stupid. I know what goes on. I'll ask some of the old lags, cabbies, in the markets, people I know.'

'Well, I don't want no trouble. It's one thing bringing him here for her to look after. Another getting involved in this racket. Have you met some of these types? Nobs, judges, coppers, the lot. Money and power, mate. Take my advice and leave it alone.'

'I'm not talking about the law, just a taste of their own medicine, a duffing up . . . He's just a kid . . .'

They look down at him.

'Still had no business selling his ass. I never did.'

'He's just a kid.'

'Yea, well it ain't right. Plenty of other ways to get some dosh.'

'Some people just crumble, nothing inside them, nothing good ever given them, they give way, rot from the inside.'

'Should top himself then . . .'

Candida watches him sleeping, he is frowning and muttering. He is all dusty and bruised and bleeding. She aches to pick him up and nurse him. But knows better. He is probably an angry little tyke, bitter or broken. There is no way of telling which. On the radio she once heard a doctor talk about torture. He had said, that, if they lived, people came out either broken, their spark out, or almost unaffected, as though their bodies might be crushed and beaten but that their spirit stayed bright. She'd seen that in the squats. Some were the walking dead who became junkies or alcoholics and went on the game and died sooner or later, whilst others were angry, bitter, cruel maybe, but they fought back and got on with their lives. And you could never tell which it would be.

'Okay, who wants breakfast?'

'No, I must be going . . .'

'No, eat something after the shock, come on . . .'

In the kitchen the chaos is reassuring. She fries eggs, makes a pile of toast (the bread was in the fridge) and a new pot of tea.

They sit down to eat. Toast, marmalade, fried eggs, pickle, hot strong tea. Blissful, solid breakfast. No one speaks. Their feeding is focused, intense, concentrated.

They finish and sit back.

'He can stay here until he gets better. Does he have friends or some one who might be worried?'

'Not that I know of. I doubt it. Lives in the tunnels, but hasn't been there long. Think he's a Londoner . . .'

'Okay.'

'I'll be back this evening . . . just to see him. Is that okay?'

'Yea.'

'Thanks,' Bill says, looking at the bloke.

'What else could I do?'

Bill looks at him. Even though it had been an effort to get him to help. He could have run on. He'd do him a turn.

'Yea, cheers mate.' He claps him on the shoulder.

'Thanks love, we'll talk.'

He walks over to the boy. 'I'll get those bastards, kid. Trust your Uncle Bill.'

The boy is out cold.

He smiles grimly and picks up his coat.

'Here, let me brush it down.' She takes it from him and inspects it. A few muddy patches but none the worse for wear. She takes it into the kitchen and dabs it with a wet cloth. He puts on his coat and leaves.

The bloke is in the bathroom. Candida takes some large, flat cushions and her duvet and lies down near the sleeping boy. She had a bad night. The food has sedated her. Soon she is sleeping. Their breaths coalesce as they sink further and further away.

When he comes out of his bath they are both out cold. He gives them a quick look and then he slips out into the daylight. Sod the charity, he has a deal to do.

Chapter Twelve

Elsie drifts into a troubled sleep. The drug precludes proper rest, but provides a grey, twilight oblivion, where the muscles relax, the jaw unclenches and soft emptiness envelopes her. As she dozes, thoughts tumble around.

Her heart has been playing up; she wonders if this is all too much. But then why preserve the flesh for the sake of preservation? Better to go out singing and dancing. She'd seen the old women bent double, painfully shuffling the streets, wearing carpet slippers, stained and rumpled clothes and mumbling to themselves. She dreads sinking so far and prays she will go before things get so bad.

There is no one to care for her if she does go senile. No children, no family to speak of. She'd been brought up around St Pancras but the bombs had put paid to her manor. People had scattered, died, moved up or down. Either way they'd drifted. Her brother had died in the desert, they weren't close in any case, she'd hardly missed him.

She'd never had many friends. People thought she was stuck up, and she was particular about who she mixed with. But she was more shy than snooty. Not being pretty she'd never had the confidence. Her body was good, but she had a horse face, big teeth, long, fleshy nose, mousey hair. Nice legs though, which gave her work in the clubs while she was young. Soho mainly, some variety, the odd summer season. Nothing special. Her whole life had been that: nothing special.

That's where she'd met Bill. He did magic tricks. For adults, and, later, when the work dried up, for rich kiddies' parties. He was good, could pull doves and eggs and feathers out of unlikely places. They'd done a summer season, Weymouth was it or Bournemouth? And hit it off. He was a Londoner, too, and they'd drifted together, the minor acts of the back end of the pier show.

They said his wife had died in an accident. He had a sadness about him, always held himself back. Never saw him with another woman. Once or twice he'd got soft and sentimental with her, not pushy, more pathetic. She didn't fancy him, never had. They were too alike. She liked small fleshy men. He was too thin and bony, needed something to get hold of.

They'd met on and off over the years. She didn't know much about his life now, except that he was living in the tunnels, although he had a perfectly good flat. Or perhaps he had lost it. Bill was a mystery. He had got involved in some weird religion and had gone a bit simple. He said he was conducting an experiment, a social experiment. Living with the rejects. It was above her head, she didn't understand him. He was good. She could see that, kind, gentle, but no walkover. He'd hung around with some rough boys in his day, but had never got involved. Drank with them, she supposed. He was a lovely dancer. She had quite a soft spot for him. She'd miss him if he went.

And her cats, her babies, she'd miss them, but would they miss her? Probably not. As long as they got fed they would probably hardly notice.

She slips deeper into unconsciousness. Suddenly she wakes up. Her heart is thudding, dangerously. It is the coke. She'll have to cut it out, but how? The smoke was never like this. She'd feel drowsy for a day or so but have beautiful dreams. Dreams of colours and textures, of the sea, of dancing out in the moonlight. The dreams were better than the day. Always. But her habit had stayed in a protected corner of her life. Enclosed, secret, controlled. This stuff, which she is beginning to resent, was creeping out of that safe corner, had got out, if she was honest. And she wasn't sure she had the strength to push it away.

Elsie wonders if she should get help. Maybe she could ask the boys? They'll laugh at her, besides they don't know how much she is taking. She'd found another dealer, a shady looking character. He usually brought it round, deals on wheels he called it. Except for the day she'd got mugged. Then he'd told her to come, it wasn't his day for deliveries.

She lies flat. Her heart flops and gallops. She will have to stop. A vice-like tightness encircles her chest. She wonders if she is going to have a heart attack, but it eases. She turns over on to her left side. The bones dig into the mattress; she is getting too thin. Her appetite has gone, and anyway she has never been a great eater. As she lies a tabby comes up and sits by her face, purring as if to encourage her.

It is late, they want their breakfast, she can feel their rumblings. Several leap down from the bed and there is a pacing and clattering and mewing starting up.

Mercifully the pain eases. She rolls back and sits up, supported by the pillows. Relief. If she dies here, she might end up being eaten by her own moggies. She is boss as long as she provides the food. Once that stops by sheer force of numbers they could overwhelm her. But it will not happen today.

She pulls the edge of the curtain and inspects the day. Dull, grey, damp. She lets the curtain fall back. It is now that she'd like tea and toast in bed. Well maybe just the tea.

'Any one of you lot fancy making me a cup of tea?'

The cats look up expectantly, blankly. The ginger tom jumps up on the bed and steps on her chest, nudges her under her chin. She pushes him away. Just then there is a tapping on the window.

She leans over and pulls back the curtain. It is Alice, her neighbour and partner in crime. She slips up the window and hands out the keys. Alice will make her tea and toast and anything. Alice loves her!

Letting herself in the room Alice admonishes Elsie. 'Still in bed you lazy bitch! Do you know what time it is? And the babies not fed! Well, well, it's just as well I popped in.'

She leans over to kiss her.

Standing back she says, 'You look peaky. You been taking drugs, Elsie?' It is supposed to be a joke.

Elsie smiles weakly. 'Make us a cup of tea, Alice. I'm not feeling so hot!'

'You're not going to die on me are you?' Alice is concerned. There is something up, she knows it. They've been friends since before the War, both showgirls, none too successful. She'd married, Elsie stayed single. Thankfully Alfred had gone off and she had been left in sweet peace. The person she'd really loved all these years had been Elsie, but she'd wanted kiddies so she'd put up with Arthur and his puffing and panting. As it turned out, she couldn't have them and she went sour on him. He left, following some Irish tart; she'd never seen him since.

She loved Elsie but wasn't so sure of the cats. This place stank! She'd been on at her to stop taking them in, but Elsie had a soft heart when it came to animals. People she was not so sure of. Elsie is a cool one. She'd taken to getting paid for it, after the jobs dried up. Alice had been shocked. Although they'd seen everything working in tatty clubs, she'd never expected Elsie, who was once so fastidious, to end up that way. But you never can tell.

Remembering Elsie's cleanliness she looks around the dingy room. No duster had been seen for months. The stench of cat is suffocating. Is she going downhill? She is afraid. Life without Elsie would be unbearable. She has to take her in hand. She thinks of her own neat, spick-and-span flat. No, this is disgusting.

She fills the kettle, the cats mass around her ankles weaving and crossing.

'These bloody cats! How do you stand it? The stink, the mess.' She crosses the room and pushes up the great sash window. 'Right you lot. *Out*!!' With a broom she pushes and sweeps the cats out. They understand. She is not a friend. Some hide under the bed, or on top of the old wooden wardrobe behind the armchair. Two perch like statues on the old brown radio set. The majority slither out of the window. Disperse into the scrubby front yard. They sit on and between the dustbins preening themselves in the watery morning light.

'Shut the window. It's freezing.'

'Not 'till I've got the smell of these animals out of here! I'll turn on the fire, Elsie. It niffs in here.'

Elsie looks sheepishly around the room: things have fallen behind. She doesn't seem to have the will anymore, doesn't bloody care what happens. She is used to Alice chucking the cats out, her friend is not a cat person but perhaps there are too many? She likes the company and their furry presence. They make her laugh and they are far better entertainment than any telly. But it is true the place stinks.

'Come on, get out of bed and help me.'

Alice is a frenzy of activity, Elsie sinks back into the pillows and watches her as she starts dragging the hoover across the dirty carpet. Alice is still pretty. She had been a strawberry blonde; now it is powdery white, cut longish with soft curls. Age suits her; she is plumpish but not fat and has a beautiful pink and white complexion. She is small; they used to complain in the clubs about her height. But she'd smile and they'd hire her anyway as she was pretty. The punters liked her smile. She married that ugly bloke, Elsie never knew why. Suspected it was because she was in the club. Alice was not one for the men. In fact Elsie was sure she'd had a girlfriend several years back. Nothing was said, mind you. She never knew what happened to her. Nancy? Was she called Nancy or Patsy?

The kettle boils. Elsie wants her tea, but is not sure she can make it; she feels weak and dizzy and her heart still lurches. She wants tea in bed not a bloody full-scale overhaul.

'I just want my tea,' she mouths to Alice.

Alice stops the hoover. 'Sorry, I got carried away. You do look poorly. Want me to call the doctor? You're a funny grey colour.'

'No, please, just the tea and could you shut the window? I know the place is a state, I've not been myself recently.'

There is a knock on the door. Alice looks at her friend questioningly.

'Answer it, will you?'

It is one of the Hammer Horrors. Alice gasps, she has seen them before, but never so close up. She obviously thinks he is an axe murderer.

'Sorry, could I borrow some milk?'

'Hello, Pete.'

'Hello.' He steps into the flat gingerly, Alice regarding him with great suspicion.

'Are you sick?' His nose wrinkles at the smell. It smells of age and decay and damp and cat food. He likes incense himself.

'It's a bit high here. You're right. I'm not so good.'

'Can I do something?' Pete asks, sure of a refusal.

Alice eyes this unpromising specimen. What was there that he could possibly do? 'Know how to use one of these?' She nods towards the hoover.

'Oh, yes, my girlfriend makes us do it.'

'Well then . . .'

'Thing is we've got a rehearsal . . . could I just have the milk?'

'Let the boy go, Alice.'

Alice smiles a frozen smile and opens the fridge. There is no milk.

'Where might one find this milk?'

'Oh, on the doorstep, dearie, run and fetch it will you?'

Relieved he slips out and comes back with a pint.

'Half each, but bring it back later or I'll run out.'

'Sure, thanks.'

'The tea is well brewed and Alice pours it into two mugs. She sits on the bed by her old friend, and watches her colour come back.

It is cold, cold and damp. 'Can't you get the council to get you a nice new flat? This place is damp Elsie, I can feel it in my bones.'

'Put the fire on, it'll take the chill off.'

'I'm worried about you. Do you want to come and stay at my place for a few days?'

'And bring my cats with me? No dear, I'll be fine. I didn't get much sleep. This tea will do me.'

'I came to ask you if you wanted to come to the club this afternoon . . . but you don't look well enough for dancing.'

'Think I'll give it a miss. Today I feel my age, Alice. I'm tired.'

Would you like me to stay with you? I will if you want?'

'Yes, I'd like that. Stay a while. Let's put the radio on and have a natter.'

Chapter Thirteen

Bill walks stiffly down the street. His tiredness has left him and his movements are fuelled by a slow burning rage. He is thinking about the boy; he is just a kid after all; what chance did he have? He'd met these geezers, they all had. They give him the creeps. The boy hadn't said much, he'd looked at the bloke and wasn't clear whether he trusted him or not. But if he was for sale, it couldn't have been the first time this had happened, after all rape was an occupational hazard. But why had he been dumped like that, so publicly? Perhaps they had been surprised, whoever they were; he'd assumed there had been more than one, the boy would have fought one man off. He'd go round a few taxi drivers and see if anyone knew anything. But the bloke was right. What will he do even if he does find out? If it's a ring then he'd better forget it, they would all be in it, cops, lawyers, judges, social workers.

He goes under the bridge and down the traffic-choked road. The cars sit bumper to bumper. People huddle in clutches at the bus stops, against a cold sharp wind that blows across them. The place has been getting smellier and dirtier. It is run down. The economic miracle has definitely passed Camden by. There are some smart office blocks but mostly there is decay, poverty, dirt.

The winos in the tube station are at their posts. Some are in rags, others on crutches. Black eyes, broken noses, cracked voices, they are the end of the line. The stench permeates the surrounds. People circle them widely. A dishevelled woman, her florid face blackened by ingrained dirt, asks drunkenly for some money. Bill side-steps her too. He never gives to drunks. The woman curses him as he passes; she is swaying alarmingly. Out of the tube he crosses the High Street and walks into the market. It is still early and many of the stalls are not set up yet. He goes to the café; they are probably having breakfast.

The café is steaming with bodies and the tea urn. Condensation runs down the walls. A welcoming smell of fried bacon and sausages fills the air. He has, however, not come to eat.

'Gladys, is Arthur here?'

'He's over there, Bill.'

Arthur is sat in a group at the back of the café with a couple of cabbies. Great! Two birds with one stone. Bill greets them and, taking a chair from a nearby table, sits down. Gladys sets down a mug of strong tea. They acknowledge him without speaking and carry on their conversation.

It isn't a conversation, more a London moan. High prices, no work, hassling coppers, terrible traffic, awful passengers, foul weather . . . The familiar, reassuring litany. Bill listens to this ritual, watching their faces. They are okay. They moan, but they are comfortable. Most of them have bought their council houses, some in very bijoux spots in the East End. Their living isn't as good as it has been, but they have nothing important to worry about. Their money doesn't make them happier, though. He doesn't envy them their secure lives; they are like hamsters in a wheel whizzing round, going nowhere.

'Did any of you pick up a man and a boy last night? Drop them in Regent's Park?'

'Why?'

'Someone I know got done over, in the park.'

'Oh.' The lack of interest is disappointing but predictable. 'Ask Gladys.'

She is called over and asked the same question. She blanches and then reddens, her eyes narrowing. 'Why do you want to know?'

'A friend of mine . . . got hurt.'

She motions him to come over to one side of the café. 'Listen. Are you crazy! Asking questions like that?'

'A friend of mine . . .'

'You know the score. Leave it alone!'

'So you have heard something?'

'Things go on. You know that. You also know what happens when people stick their noses in. Bill, don't be an idiot. These guys would eat you for breakfast. No trouble. I know. We get all sorts in here. Get down off your white horse. Leave it.'

'It's just not right that they should get away with it.'

'Where are you living, Bill? Fairyland? Whoever said it was right?'

'Maybe you're right. I'll fight back another way.'

'Don't fight back at all, Bill. Forget it.'

Her face relaxes and the heavy frown line eases on her forehead. She wipes her hands on her apron and looks at him, head on one side. 'Take care of yourself, we'd hate to lose you, Bill.'

'Yea, don't worry.'

He turns to leave the café when he catches the eye of a woman cabbie sitting alone. She is weighing him up. He stops, and then deliberately walks outside. The market is filling up. Shoppers, browsers and pickpockets mingle. The sun is trying bravely, but only a thin streak of light penetrates the gloom. He stands in front of the flower stall. He's always loved flowers, their colours radiate hope, beauty and hope. Best of all he loves lilies, the deep scent they give off at night, their glorious waxy petals and little floury stems which trail stuff like curry powder.

The woman cabby is standing beside him. A real butch type if he's ever seen one. Small and stocky, short hair, fairly plain face, wearing an old tweed jacket and rumpled men's trousers.

She extends her hand. 'Pat.'

'Bill.' He shakes her hand.

They walk slowly through the market.

'I overheard you . . .'

'A friend of mine . . .'

'Young black kid?'

'Yes !'

'I picked them up outside the gay café, near Tottenham Court

Road. Last night, around ten, no, maybe earlier. A boy and a man in a suit. Looked well-off, upper class. Civil servant or banker, that type. Didn't talk to each other. I watched because they were a strange couple. Didn't go together, if you get my drift. Dropped them off by the park, Inner Circle. Is he hurt? Dead?' She seems strangely detached.

She is aware of Bill's distaste for what she has said and continues.

'Look. You see it all, driving a cab. People think they're invisible. We see all sorts of stuff.'

'I'm not blaming you. It's just he's a kid.'

'So he's alive?'

'Just. Listen, thanks. The less you know the better.'

'Damn right. I'm not getting involved. Just thought I'd do you a favour.'

'Well, thanks. I really appreciate it. If there's ever . . .'

'Yeah, well take care. Like the lady said, they're mean bastards.'

'Thanks.'

He suddenly feels tired. Shattered. He'll go to the park and have a kip. On second thoughts, it is cold. He'll try the library. He turns into the High Street and slowly weaves his way through the crowds. Pat the cabby watches him. She hopes she's done the right thing and that he doesn't end up with trouble he can't handle. In the end though, sometimes you just have to stick your neck out, or else nothing ever changes. She'll light a candle for him. Poor old sod.

Chapter Fourteen

They awake together. A spear of sunlight has pierced the blinds and landed near their heads. They gasp as they see each other, then remember and both drop their gaze. Candida's tear-filled eyes meet his a second time.

'How are you?'

'Hungry.'

'And?'

'I hurt.' Her tears draw his and, despite his trying not to cry, his lip quivers and tears overflow and run rushing down his face. He lays his head down and weeps. Noiselessly his body shudders. She moves over to him and lays her arm across him. He stops suddenly.

'It's okay. You're safe here.'

But at her touch he has clammed up. His heart aches and his throat is sore from swallowing. He drags himself up.

'Do you want a bath?'

'Yea.' The hardness returns.

'Listen, you can stay here as long as you like. It's okay.'

'Really?' He clearly doesn't believe her.

'I'll run the bath. No, I want some tea first. Tea and toast?'

'I need to wash . . .'

'Yes, of course. Right. But tea, tea we will have.'

She gets up and shambles into the bathroom. Turning the hot tap she instinctively reaches for the sandalwood oil. Then stops herself. Perhaps he won't like it. She puts it in anyway, cleansing, healing, sandal. Perhaps some . . . ylang ylang? No, too sweet. Melissa, melissa would be perfect for putting it all back together, well to start the process, calming, soothing, opening the heart. She sighs. Pretty impossible, God knows what kind of life he's had to have ended up here. And how he must feel now. Still, be practical, don't let him have to deal with your feelings on top of everything else.

The hot water gushes in the tub. She lights two candles she keeps by the bath. They are new, long, blue and silky. She turns off the light and stands in the darkness, and feels the calm peace that candlelight brings.

She goes into her bedroom and puts on a cassette. Something mournful, Celtic, some Irish lament. Its incandescent lilt and the fragrance from the bath mingle.

The boy has dropped off again. She touches him lightly on his shoulder and he jerks up.

'Your bath, it's running.' He gets up slowly, stiffly. He is embarrassed and hides it with bravado.

'You got some clothes I can borrow? A towel?'

He follows her as she walks toward the bathroom.

'What's that smell? It's lovely, smells like summer, like trees.'

'Sandalwood and melissa. I put them in your bath. They'll make you feel better.'

His face collapses. Nothing will make him feel better. Ever. She watches him.

'They will, promise.'

He shrugs. The spell broken.

'Here's a towel. I'll see if I can find you some clothes. He is about the same size as the bloke. She goes into the bedroom to look.

The boy closes the bathroom door. He stands in the candlelight. It is like being in church. Holy. And the smell is like incense. He loves churches, their dank mustiness is reassuring. And people sing there and they pray. He prayed sometimes. He prayed last night. Prayed, what had he prayed? He can't remember. He knows he prayed for something, but can't tell if his prayer has been answered. Maybe he should pray now. He kneels down by the tub. He sees the level of the water rising and reaches to turn the tap off.

'God, get me out of this.'

His prayer is short and to the point. Then he thinks this . . . what? 'God, change my life.'

He isn't happy with this either. He might change it for the worse. 'God, make my life better.'

That's it! He wants a better life.

'God, make my life better. Make me not die from AIDS.'

Fat chance. Still with prayer, everything is possible. A priest had told him. Not that they told the truth any more than anyone else. But he knew inside that the priest was right.

'God, let me not die from AIDS.'

She knocks on the door and an arm comes through with a pile of clothes. He takes them and examines them. A pair of jeans, Levi's. A brushed cotton lumberjack shirt, socks, underwear. He puts them carefully in a pile on the floor. He stands in front of the long mirror. It is a shock. He is a mess. It is months since he has seen his whole self in a real mirror. Mostly seen the head and shoulders in café mirrors, in the gents. Has seen his murky outline reflected in shop windows. The image is dulled by the candlelight, but here he is whole and it is horrible. He turns away, but turns back. Fascination, horror. He's grown tall and thin, but muscles have appeared. The soft flesh of his childhood has disappeared.

But his face! The lip is swollen and split at one corner, a scratch runs down one side, the other has a graze, like on gravel. His eyes are puffy and swollen and bloodshot. The white bits are red and streaked. His hair is matted, small locks are poking up but he has half the park ground into them. His clothes are torn. He feels surreal. He slides them off and stands naked in front of the mirror. A candle gutters. His skin is mottled in places. Bad food does that. He twists around. Nothing, a few scratches. The marks are inside.

He looks at the bathroom. It is full of shells, she must collect them. It is painted a bright blue and is large. The woodwork is silver and a bit chipped. Someone has stencilled stars and moons across the walls and a vase holds peacock feathers. Lots of dark blue glass jars run along a red painted shelf. He likes the feel of the place.

He runs some cold water and then steps into the bath. It is hot but it makes him shiver. Inside he is frozen. He slowly lets himself down into the steaming water. He lays backwards and lets the weight of the water hold his aching muscles, his sore bones. He closes his eyes, and for the first time becomes aware of the music. It is like seagulls and early morning before the city wakes. Misty, cold, but safe. The oils work, unravelling, soothing.

She puts her head around the door.

'Want some tea? I won't look.'

He answers drowsily.

'Don't fall asleep, you'll drown. There's lots of hot water, you can wash in this one and then run another to just lie in.'

She is great! She knows what he is thinking. The soap smells too, vanilla maybe. This is a dream. Maybe it is his prayer!

Although it can't last. Depression slumps him.

She comes in with the tea, avoiding looking at him.

'You can stay as long as you like, I told you.'

'You'll get fed up with me. Everyone does.'

'Why do they?'

'Dunno.'

'Are you violent?' She remembers the dog/rat.

'Sometimes, only when . . . only when . . . it gets too much.' It is then that he realises there is silence in his head. He listens carefully. No noise; there has been no noise since he woke up. He remembers, they had stopped buzzing last night.

'What?'

'Nothing.'

She looks at him. He looks away, ashamed he won't trust her. But he won't. Not with that, he'd never told anyone about the flies, it would make them real. She might have him locked up. Not yet. Maybe he'll tell her some day. Already he is thinking he might know her. He smiles a tiny smile. Looking at her.

'Thanks, I'm going to wash now.'

She leaves. He calls after her, 'The music, it's lovely. Thank you for all this. No one has ever . . .'

'I know.'

Chapter Fifteen

Uther wakes late. Bad tempered, he sits at the table. The ash tray is full. There are two cups and the remains of the cake piled up by his elbow. He tries to remember why she stormed off but his brain is foggy with sleep. He shrugs, there are more where she came from. Women like him, he rarely sleeps alone. He loves women, all shapes and sizes and colours. He likes to be around their softness, they make him feel like a man, something he has trouble with when he compares himself to other men. He is a big sissy really, only his size stops him being picked on. He feels like a lumbering bear, genial, eager to please, winsome. He hates physical pain and will do and say almost anything to avoid it.

He sighs; that is the beginning and end of his troubles. Women, he chases them, beds them wherever and whenever he can; they appear in shops, on street corners, in cafés, and especially when he is playing, women go crazy for musicians, they just line up. How could he say no? He doesn't. He loves them, Jane has cried and threatened to leave him, wheedled, blackmailed but none of it makes any difference. He can't help himself, helping himself.

He smiles, he's seen a chick around the corner he quite fancies; they'd met in the supermarket one morning. He'd smiled his special smile and she'd smiled shyly back. Shy women drove him crazy, their little secret tentative glances, they were often the wildest in bed, all that repressed energy. He shakes himself. He'd find her. She lives in one of the old houses by the Park. That will take his mind off the last one, what was her name?

Uther is in London to work. There is no work in Cornwall. They'd stripped the mines and quarries and taken the money out. Even the fishing is bad. He comes during the winter months in his bus; he plays the clubs and pubs at night and by day he takes labouring work, whatever he can find. Sometimes he does the markets for a friend: Camden, Portobello, Greenwich. It is hard but means he has the summer in his bus to live an uncomplicated nomadic life.

He has a gig tonight and needs to prepare his songs, but his mind is distracted, scattered. On bad days he wonders where he'll end up. Not like his father, he hopes. His dad had been a tin miner, and when those had closed down, he'd tried fishing. He couldn't adapt though, and was a misery for several years before he died quickly, cleanly almost, of cancer. His mother had followed two years later. Died of a broken heart, he reckons. One morning she just didn't get up and when he had called in, lunch time, she was laid out, smiling a secret smile on their bed.

He had been excluded by them; his parents were devoted to each other, had not wanted children. He was a mistake, as his father had let slip in a row. Uther had known in any case. He was a changeling. Didn't resemble any of his family. His parents were small, dark, secretive Cornish people. He was tall, golden skinned, freckled. He didn't know why they had called him Uther. His mother had had a romance with Arthurian legends and had read him to sleep with Lancelot and Guinevere from when he was a small child. Perhaps it had been a joke. They hadn't taken him that seriously, as a child or a man. When he had become a wanderer they had called him feckless. If he met his father out with his friends, he would pretend not to see him. Uther had embarrassed both of them.

Uther had tried to settle down. Got himself a job in the parks, found a nice woman and had two kids. They had lived in a house on an estate and had lasted just long enough to birth the children. Suffocated, he had run. His mother never forgave him. But his wife understood. She had found a better provider and had another couple of children. His two were assimilated into the new family and he was told it was better he didn't visit. They were all relieved when he moved away.

Sometimes he thought about the children, but a teaspoon of sperm does not make a father. His wife was a sensible woman, kind in a limited way, they'd be fine with her. If they wanted an eccentric father when they grew up he would be there for them. But somehow he doubted they would.

This is his sixth year of exile. He feels it is more dignified to do manual work than to sign on and sit winter out as a passive claimant. He believes it rots the soul. Perhaps the system was designed that way. The demeaning queues, the bored and faintly sadistic counter staff, the disapproving woman at the post office where you cashed the cheque. Tainted money. It poisoned the recipients, making them apathetic, self-hating, and above all, passive.

Uther had left Cornwall and hitched up to London, found a place in a squat and started playing the pubs and folk clubs. He'd met Jane in one, working behind the bar. She was frantic to get out of London, so they'd pooled their money and bought the bus from a man her father knew. He'd taught Uther how to take care of it and introduced him to a whole network of men with buses. There were bus collectors all over the country. They met at bus rallies and anxiously tinkered with their engines, driving them sedately along quiet roads.

They were mostly older men who showed him their buses with paternal pride. When things went wrong they would drive long distances to help him out. Breaking down was a constant worry; the only thing that could tow a bus was another bus. But these men had their contacts with the bus companies and a few phone calls would bring out a spare part or a trained mechanic. Buses were their lives, their passion. The blue bus had brought Uther a new family.

That first year had been the happiest. They'd met so many friendly people on the road, there was a real feeling of comradeship. They were welcomed and fêted when people found they were musicians and had sat around hundreds of night fires singing for their supper, drinking strong country ale and getting stoned. It had been a magic time.

The winter had been hard. They drove around trying to find a place to settle and were moved on again and again. Often late at night when the local coppers had nothing better to do they'd swoop down and start banging the side of the bus, frightening the hell out of them. They'd have to get up and drive off, across the county line, however little sleep they'd had.

This split life, though, had its cost. Friendships were stretched and sometimes fractured beyond repair. He felt he belonged to nothing. London hardened him. He grew sharp edges, a caustic tongue, became more insulated, hostile. When he returned home it took four weeks at least to pick the barbs and prickles off his skin. He had to shake himself like a dog out of water before he could slip into his Cornish skin. Then Jane would start getting restless and they'd hit the road: Wales, Devon, Shropshire, Norfolk.

The second year they met more people, their name had passed around. Their circle grew and grew and they got on the festival network. Jane made cakes and sold them, he played his music. They began to earn good money, enough to keep repairing the bus, but in winter they had to work or live abroad, somewhere cheap. Jane wanted to travel: Bali, India, South America, but Uther hated the sun and felt anchored to Britain. He wanted to be in Cornwall. London is a bad compromise. There is lots of music here but he hates cities. Jane wants the sun but gets excitement from city frenzy. In truth he is tired of travelling. The novelty has worn off and he wants to put down roots, get a place by the sea, settle again. But Jane doesn't like Cornwall and refuses to consider it. They've had countless rows about it, but neither of them will give way. They have reached the point of splitting up, but no one wants to make the first move. Jane has gone to stay with her sister, to think things over.

Uther sits down on the step of the bus with his tin whistle and plays a Breton song, morosely. A fine rain is falling, through the railings he can see the soaked grass of the hill, coarse and tufted. Two jagged hawthorns, bent and twisted by the hill top winds sway slightly by the falling rain. It is cold and dull. Slate grey, pale green, with patches of black. To his left the sun is edging out from behind a solid mass of cloud. The cold doesn't trouble him, he is used to all weathers, the Cornish winter could be as bleak, but somehow the dreariness of the city aggravates the chill. Uther gets up from the step and goes back into the bus. He considers tidying up but can't be bothered. He thought about the girl in the supermarket and decides he'll have a wander around and see if his luck has changed.

Chapter Sixteen

☾

While he is bathing Candida sits in the kitchen. She has the oven on to heat the room and is leaning on her elbows sitting at the table. A mug of tea sits beside her, growing cold. She has said he can stay. His disbelief pressed her to urge him to take her up on her offer. She does not understand how she has managed to not eject one man and to find another one as well. It is not even ten-thirty!

The panther stands beside her, his neck bent and his head resting on her lap. She strokes it absentmindedly. Now what? He might stay for days, weeks, months? And the bloke, how can she throw him out? She sighs hopelessly. How can things change from one to another so quickly and irrevocably? And why is she left holding the baby? The music stops. She walks into her bedroom and turns the cassette over. As she passes the bathroom she can hear the boy humming. She is pleased he is enjoying her bath and decides she will make a cake. It will give her head space while she decides what she is going to do.

Mentally she makes a list: eggs, sugar, butter, flour, carob, ground almonds, yes, she has the lot. She sets to work humming and weighs out the butter, unsalted, pale, oily, and the thick muscovado sugar. She puts them in a glazed earthenware bowl and begins beating them with a wooden spoon, slowly, holding the bowl in the crook of her left arm. When they are creamed the mixture becomes grainy because of the thick sugar and turns a rich dark molasses colour. She separates the eggs and slowly folds in the egg yolks until the mixture is deep and creamy. She whisks the egg whites for a long time until they stand up in bubbly peaks. She weighs the carob and flour and slowly mixes them all in with the ground almonds until it is a thick, heavy dough. A teaspoon of almond essence is added as an afterthought.

The boy appears like a phantom at the doorway. He is wearing the bloke's clothes and seems a little more alive, but he is thin, malnourished, his skin dull, with no lustre. His baby dreadlocks leap and bounce out of his head, water drips off them, on to his shirt.

'Come in, sit down. I'm making a cake.'

His eyes widen.

'Come on! You're making me nervous standing there.'

He walks cautiously, no, sidles around the edges of the kitchen and sits painfully on the chair.

'Tea?'

'Yes. I'm hungry. Do you have . . . ?'

'Toast, eggs?'

'Everything.'

She smiles, maybe he isn't going to be such a pain after all, he might even be good company.

'Let me put the cake in. The tea's on the table.'

He watches her. Bending down rattling about in the cupboard looking for cake tins. Sort of mumsy she is. He likes the idea of cake. The kitchen is bright, neat and warm. God it is warm. He had drifted off in the bath briefly but the coldness of the water brought him back to consciousness. He had dressed in the new clothes, which fit him perfectly. He admired his restored self in the mirror. The clothes did it, although his face is still a mess. He feels stronger and pours his tea.

'This your place?'

'No, rented.'

'Nice.'

'Yea, I like it. The neighbours are okay. No loud parties, no screaming rows, they're quiet but friendly.' She is spooning the mixture lovingly into two tins. He dips his finger into the bowl and licks it.

'Not bad!'

She tries some too, pretending it is for the first time. 'I'd say!'

He dips his finger in again. God he is hungry.

'No more!'

'I'm hungry.'

'The sooner you let me get it in the oven, the sooner you'll get breakfast.'

She grins at him, he smiles uncertainly back.

'Can you cook?'

'No, I've never learnt.'

'Well, I'll have to teach you.'

'Look, you don't have to put me up, it's okay.'

'I know I don't have to, but until we find you somewhere else, stay here.'

'Somewhere else?'

'A place of your own. Why not?'

'I've never had . . .'

'I know, but that doesn't mean you can't.'

'I suppose.' He doesn't believe her. Things like this are not possible. He belongs to the tunnels. To filth and pain and hopelessness. He looks away. Tears well up again. He said, that bloke had said that he didn't deserve to live and he was right! Trash. His father had told him too, and his mum. They knew.

She watches as his face puckers and hardens. Thoughts are rippling across his face. He looks so young, but she will never catch up on the things he's seen and done. He feels battered and old, almost used up. A solitary tear escapes and he brushes it angrily to one side. He turns away and bends over as if ashamed. She is watching him, undecided what to do. If she goes to him he'd resent it, if she ignores him, the same. She stands looking at her feet.

He watches her through his eyelashes. He hates people to see him like this. But she hasn't tried to make him better, which is a relief, or to shut him up. The music stops. She leaves the room and he sits back again. But this hurts too much, so he sits forward, leaning his head on his hands. He can smell cake. He is smiling as she comes back into the room.

'I don't know your name.'

'Mark.'

'I'm Candida.'

'Funny name.'

'I know, but I think it suits me.'

'Why?'

She smiles, 'Because, because, oh I don't know. Because it's my name.'

'I'd like an African name.'

'Is that where you're from?'

'No, Kilburn!' He laughs at the absurdity. 'But my dad's African, he's from . . . Nigeria I think?'

She looks sceptical.

'Nah, he's from Kilburn too!' He laughs, leaning back. He stops suddenly with the pain.

'Does it hurt?'

'Yes.' His voice has gone low and weak again. 'It hurts a lot.'

'How old are you?'

'Fifteen.' She pulls a face. 'Fourteen, well . . . thirteen actually. Fourteen in November.'

He looks at her appealingly, this is dangerous ground.

'How long . . . ?'

'Six months, longer, end of the summer. My old man threw me out.'

'Why?'

'Dunno.'

'Why?'

'He doesn't like me much.'

'You in trouble?'

'Yea.' He is getting restless now. Wants to run. His reflexes are screaming: *Get out*!

'It's okay. Calm down. I ran away too.'

'You did?'

'Me and a million others. It doesn't make you so special.'

He blinks back at her.

'The world is full of runaways. It's no big deal. Now let's eat.'

She sets about toasting bread and frying eggs. He watches her impressed. Maybe his prayer has got answered.

She'd never wanted kids, there were enough orphans on the streets. They made her maternal, she even felt bodily twinges. He is like one of those greedy chicks in a blackbird's nest, chirruping angrily, full of demands, insistent, having no hope of being heard. He swings wildly between the two extremes. She watches him wolf down three fried eggs and a mound of toast running with butter. Greedy for warmth and nourishment. She can see a flush of colour on his lips. He gulps his mug of tea and looks around for more.

'More?' Smiling, 'Toast?'

She cuts the rest of the bread, almost a whole loaf gone, and toasts it. They sit and butter the toast and spread thick, chunky, dark marmalade on top. Finally, sated, they sit back. He yawns. The warm bath and all the food has exhausted him.

'Go back to bed, sleep again, sleep is healing. You can sleep in my bed out of the way. Come! I'll show you.'

She takes his hand, it is limp as he follows her out of the kitchen.

'What is it?'

'Nothing.' He looks away.

She picks up the duvet and leads him into her bedroom. The curtains are drawn from the night before, the hazy light shows a small and cosy room, painted a deep crimson. In the centre is a large brass bedstead. Scattered around the bed and falling on to the floor are cushions of white lace and broderie anglaise in different sizes. On one side of the bed is a table with a lampshade perched amongst beads, bracelets and other clutter. Some glass beads are draped over the lampshade which has been turned off. There is a large, dark wood wardrobe. The door is open and from it bursts a cacophony of colours and fabrics; satin, velvet, furs, sequins, organdies, multi-coloured silks. At the bottom is a heap of boots, scarves and bags. The clothes make a trail across the room, bright colours, shiny, patterned surfaces. On the other side of the room is a low table with a pile of cassettes which seem to be making their way across the room to join the clothes. Some are in boxes, others loose, some have become unwound, they fall in disarray across the table and the floor. Above the cassette deck is a bookshelf. There are no books but a collection of glass jars and bottles of different colours, more scarves and earrings and bangles. There are postcards and posters heaped precariously on necklaces and empty make-up containers.

Mark stands open-mouthed absorbing it all. The few flats he has seen, mostly belonging to punters, have been sparse: chrome and leather or white and green and airy. He is entranced.

'I keep meaning to clear it up, but I hate housework.'

He walks over to a pile of clothes and picks up a coral satin shirt. He holds it to his cheek. It is so soft.

'Look, look in the mirror. There's one on the door.'

He pulls open the wardrobe door and sees himself. He throws the shirt down angrily.

'What are you doing to me! I'm not a girl!'

She steps back, shocked. Then she shrugs and says, 'The bed's there, get some sleep,' and walks out stiffly.

He stands in the middle of the room. His legs buckle and he slowly collapses on to the pile of clothes. He sobs softly, then loudly, feeling the dull, oozing pain in his heart. She hears him cry but does not come back. After a while he dozes off into a dreamless sleep.

In the kitchen the cakes are cooked. She takes the tins out of the oven and sits down by the table. She thinks about Uther and wonders if she should go and see him. But feels she can't take any more people. He will wait. Or at least she hopes he will. She is sleepy too. She decides to go out to the shops. She wonders about leaving the boy alone in the flat, there is nothing to steal. Softly she lets herself out.

Outside, she guesses it must be lunch time. The pavements are bursting with people. At the corner shop there is a large queue massed around the till. Bracing herself she enters the mêlée.

Eggs, milk, butter, bread, jam. She looks her bag, there is not much money left. That will have to do. They can have omelette for tea or pancakes. Tea. She almost forgot the tea. Taking hold of the packet she joins the queue to pay. The shop is run by a Cypriot family. Two brothers, she thinks, and their sons and daughters. The mothers she has never seen. They are friendly and not too expensive and open wonderfully long hours. She often slips in, for late night munchies, to buy hummus or corn chips and chocolate bars or mango juice and cashews. The brothers smile when she reaches the head of the queue. She has just enough money. Carrying the blue plastic bag she walks slowly back to her flat.

As she reaches the door she sees Bill standing on the top step. She has forgotten that he is coming this afternoon, perhaps it is later than she thought. She sighs. No peace. It will be a long time before she gets any peace.

Chapter Seventeen

The bloke is waiting for his man in a seedy pub in Brixton. Midday, and it is packed. Half West Indian hard men, some rastas and white guys, old boozers, young druggies and a few tarts, white, old, haggard, hanging round the old black guys. South London low life. He sits at a table watching the show. A young black woman, too thin for his liking, is taking her clothes off in a bored listless way. The men watch silently, part fascination part intimidation. There aren't many black strippers, makes the punters feel uncomfortable. She finishes and a limp applause breaks out. The crowd moves back to the bar.

He sips his lemonade. He can't drink, it makes him pass out. The man is late. Always. After this morning he is more anxious than ever to get away. Doesn't like the whole business. If Bill hadn't threatened him, he'd have kept right on running. He isn't in the business of rescuing other people. They need to look after themselves, just like he did. Anyhow, he detests that sordid world; there are other ways of making it without selling yourself. The boy would bring nothing but trouble. As for Bill thinking he can get the perverts who did it, he was kidding himself. He'd end up dead in a hedge if he wasn't careful.

The man has said it will be soon. He'll try and put pressure on him to hurry them up. He's even brought his passport, just in case. He sees him, entering the pub. Their eyes meet and he walks out again. The bloke follows him out and through the covered market into another pub. They take their drinks to the back, by the pool table.

The man is Italian he thinks, or perhaps gypsy. Probably a faggot, the place is crawling with them. They sit down. This pub is more of the old-fashioned kind. Rheumy-eyed old men in macs sit in front of their pints, a fruit machine makes electronic musical noises, the barman stares up at a television, absentmindedly polishing a glass. The place is half empty and smells of Old Holborn, sour beer, and sweat. There is no one on the pool table, probably too early for the lunchtime crowd.

They sit opposite one another, with a small rickety wooden table between them. He is wearing a thick donkey jacket of navy wool, his silky dark hair falls in ringlets. One ear has a fat golden earring, circular, in it. His face is thin and creased with deep wrinkles, smile lines; he looks like a man who has never worried. They had met accidentally; he'd been asking around, seeing if someone wanted a driver, when this bloke came up. They'd met in the pub and he'd checked him out. They'd met three times since then. Always in the same place. The bloke getting impatient, wonders if he is being spun a line.

'Well?'

'It's tonight.'

'Great.'

'Got your passport?'

'Yeah.'

'In the usual place then, about eight-thirty?'

'Okay.' The man gets up to leave. 'And the money? It's okay still?'

'Of course, these guys are loaded. Don't worry about the money. Worry about getting back, clean.'

'I'll be fine.'

'Well then.' He drinks his lager and walks out without looking back.

The bloke smiles. Finally, his luck is changing. He'll be out of here soon. Marbella, here I come!

He finishes his drink and leaves the pub. It is cold and raining steadily. There are hours to kill. He decides to see what is on at the flicks. Then he realises how hungry he is. He goes back into the market to find a place to eat. He is particular, can't take greasy fry ups. He finds a small Italian café and slips into one of the empty tables. He orders a pizza and sits back and watches the market from the window.

He is startled when a voice asks if the table is free. He looks up; it is a cabbie, he has his badge around his fat neck. He sits down and immediately strikes up a conversation.

'Haven't I seen you somewhere, mate?'

He is eyeing the bloke closely, he shifts in his seat and ignores him. This he could do without.

'You from round here?'

'No.'

'Where then? You play pool?'

'No.'

'I never forget a face . . .'

'Look mate, I don't know you, never met you, okay?'

The cabby looks at him. His pizza arrives. He attacks it ravenously, concentrating fixedly on eating, he forgets the nosey cabbie.

'I know where! This morning, dead early in the park. I picked you up with two blokes, one of them well sozzled! Yea, I remember now. He was in a right state, wasn't he, could hardly stand. And I took you to . . . let me see if I can remember . . .'

The bloke panics. 'Listen! For the last time! I've never seen you or your bloody cab before. Got it?'

He jumps up. Pushing aside his chair he walks to the till and pays, slamming the money down on the counter and rushes out of the café.

Jesus! He knew the boy was bad luck! Bloody knew it! Just as his luck is changing. As if everything is against him. He leaves the covered market and crosses the busy street, bumping and jostling the shoppers. Someone calls out after him. He doesn't believe it! The cabby is running after him, waving something.

'Stop! Stop!'

Curious passers-by halt to watch, a policeman on the beat slows down and looks over at him. He has no other choice than to stop and turn around. The last thing he wants is rozzers poking their noses into his business.

Puffing, the red-faced cabby catches up with him. He stops gasping for breath.

'Listen . . . I only wanted to say you left this in the cab . . .' He hands him a package. 'No offence mate, just thought you might want it . . .'

The bloke opens it. Inside is a gold signet ring.

'I found it on the floor of the cab when I stopped for my break.'

The ring has a Masonic seal on it. The cabby smiles complicitly.

'Thanks mate, really appreciate it.'

'No trouble. Pass it on will you.' He obviously doesn't think the bloke is Freemason material. Resentfully the bloke puts it in his pocket and walks off. The copper is still watching him, deliberating whether or not to follow him. The bloke holds his breath and jauntily walks down the street, slowly, trying to be nonchalant.

'Excuse me, sir.'

He turns around slowly.

'Officer?'

'What did that cabbie hand you?'

He takes the ring out of his pocket. 'A friend left it in his cab.'

'A friend, sir? What kind of friend might that be?'

'An old friend.' He looks blankly back. The rozzer is young and pink and baby-faced. A copper nonetheless.

'Gold is it, sir?'

'I should imagine so. It belongs to my friend.'

'Your old friend.'

'Yes.'

The copper is toying with the ring until he sees the Masonic insignia. He looks at the bloke, more doubtful than ever.

'It's not mine. My friend left it in the cab this morning. I didn't even know he was a Mason. The cabby recognised me and came chasing after me. Now I've got to go all the way to Camden to give it back.' He looks almost pleadingly at the young copper.

'Okay. But next time you're nicked. Understand?'

'Yea.'

Coming into view is the gypsy. He walks past slowly taking in the whole scene, and turns back into the market. The bloke's heart sinks. Bloody hell! Is everything against him?

The copper moves off and he walks as slowly as he dares after the gypsy. But he has gone. He feels like weeping with rage and frustration. The look on the gypsy's face has told him all he needs to know. If he loses this deal because of that boy he'll kill him! He follows the market round and comes back into the High Street. He wants to get out of here as quickly as possible before that copper changes his mind. He slips into the tube and, buying a ticket, walks down the escalator. Swallowed up by the impatient crowd he lets out a moan of frustration as he paces to and fro on the platform. The bloody boy! He'll pay for this.

Chapter Eighteen

Bill has not gone to the library. He had needed a place to think. He rode the Northern Line to Bank and then changed to the Central Line, east to Bethnal Green. After Bank he had the carriage to himself, he spread his legs wide and looked in the blackened window. There was a distortion in the glass with everything replicated three times; the bags under his eyes reached down to his prominent cheek bones. He looked old, thin, wrinkled. Deep lines cut across his forehead and down the sides of his mouth, his jaw line sagged and his neck above his knotted scarf was creased like a turkey gizzard. His hair, slate grey, was growing over his ears but he was bald on top apart from a few stray hairs which were clinging to his head. He'd lost his hat and his thick worsted coat was wearing thin and fraying at the cuffs. His shoes were cheap white trainers he'd bought in a street market, they jarred with the muted mud green colour of his clothes. He looked a mess. A musty unwashed smell came off him, mixed woodsmoke and the sulphur smell that came from the tunnels. Bristles grew on his chin; he'd missed his shave this morning and was due for a bath. He couldn't remember if the bathhouse in Bethnal Green was still open or had become a leisure centre. Maybe the monks would know.

He had come across Buddhism after his wife had been killed. He had needed some way of making sense of her horrible end. She'd survived the War, the bombs and everything, only to get run over by a bus on the Holloway Road. The senselessness of her ending haunted him. He wanted a framework to piece together the fragments of her life, they'd been together such a short time.

His mum lived alone in Canning Town surrounded by daughters, sons, grandchildren. A huge East End family. Bill was the adored baby, spoilt rotten by his seven sisters who were some of them old enough to be his mum. They worked the markets, generations of them. They were poor but comfortable.

As soon as he was able he wandered across London, east to west, north and south of the River. He walked and he watched. Bomb sites, disembowelled houses, glass shattered in piles by the roadside. He'd discovered he could dance and took to visiting the Palais whenever he had the bus fare. He'd met Kate there. Bottle blonde, blousey Kate. She'd taken a shine to him just as he accepted it as normal to have an older woman adoring him. He'd moved in with her into her little flat in Titchfield Street. His mum and sisters had come to visit. And Kate had made a grand spread, considering there was still rationing (she had connections). They gave them their blessing and consigned Bill into her capable hands.

Kate and Bill lived happily enough for seven months. He was just getting established when disaster struck. He remembered her mashed face, cold like a fish on a slab. Not much else. His sisters had done the funeral, and he'd wandered around in an agonised daze.

The banalities of life continued with hardly a pause and within weeks they'd all expected him to pick himself up and carry on. He hadn't. It was all too much. Kate had been a sensitive, she read the cards and communicated with dead spirits. Before she died she had been teaching him, said he had the gift, when she died she carried on, she was as real as ever, only he couldn't bear to see her. It hurt so.

She came in his dreams and when he wasn't thinking of much in particular. An aunt of his had read tea leaves, another had the sight, so these things were, if not normal, real enough. But it extended his grieving, it stretched over several years. His brothers tried to interest him in fishing, or football or the dogs. His mum wanted him to come back east. But he stayed in Kate's tiny flat and kept everything just as it had been. The cat left, and the budgie died a year or so later. But otherwise it was a shrine to Kate.

The dreams stopped after a while, but Kate had left him her

'power'; he could read people, see their misty auras, make sense of the lines in their hands, tell their futures. Somehow he wasn't sure this was a job for a man. His sisters came secretly for readings, and occasionally some of the old clientele turned up. One of them, Archie, was a conjurer, sozzled most of the time, he had taught Bill the rudiments of his trade and he'd worked out the rest. Bill's heart was not in this any more than 'sitting' but he felt it was a more respectable living and had done variety for years and years.

Doing magic tricks had made him a reasonable living at first, he'd liked touring, living in digs, moving on every few weeks. He did summer seasons, Brighton, Morecambe, Newquay. Bill loved the company, they'd go on great picnics on their days off, have boozy parties after the show, the chorus girls would gossip with him and he'd cheer them up when their boyfriends let them down. But he always felt detached, one step back from everyone. It was like seeing the world through a bubble. He smiled and joked, they laughed back, but he couldn't stretch out and touch them and they didn't reach him.

He was Mr Chan, the secrets of the Orient revealed. He had a beautiful turquoise costume with gold braid. A long droopy moustache and a black plait sewn to the back of his cap. He made up pointy eyes and wore panstick. The funny thing was he grew into being an Oriental. Bit by bit Mr Chan took over Bill. His cheekbones seemed to rise up on his face, his eyes narrowed and his nose, which he'd always remembered as large, appeared to shrink and flatten.

One night after the show he couldn't sleep, it was a sultry August evening. His room was suffocating, the only window was jammed shut, he couldn't catch his breath; he'd always had a touch of asthma. He put on his shirt and went out for some air. Walking along the promenade he was struck by the cobalt clouds which brooded in the darkening sky, a faint mustard glow hung over the horizon. The air was still, waiting.

He sat down on one of the wrought iron seats facing the sea. Behind him he felt a soft breeze brushing his collar, drying the sweat. He felt peculiar, light headed, all his senses were heightened. He shivered as though something was walking over his grave. He heard a whispering. At first he thought it was people walking by, but he realised it was inside him. He couldn't hear what it was saying. He tried until his head began to ache, but it was blurred like a badly tuned radio; he was sure the words were Chinese or Japanese.

He walked up and down the promenade, the noise carried on. Eventually the storm broke and he had to run for it as large juicy raindrops tore through the air. Back in his room, he dried off and lay down to sleep, lulled by the low humming noise. In the morning it had gone; he put it down to the atmospherics.

But that night when he was dozing off the voice came back. It turned out to be some kind of chanting. He took it as a sign. He started to look for a place where they worshipped like that. At first he was doubtful; in those days it was hard to find anyone interested, especially because of Japan and the War. He'd found an old Chinaman who knew a bit of meditation and the odd book in secondhand shops. He'd cobbled together his own system and as these things became more popular he'd done courses, gone to lectures and on retreats. He wasn't a Buddhist exactly, more of an eclectic; a bit of Christian mysticism, some Tantra, Patanjali, spiritualism all mixed up.

It had helped. He felt more at peace with himself. The terrible gnawing need for Kate had subsided and he fell into a contented rhythm. His beliefs set him apart. Some of his friends thought he was touched and patronised him, others, frightened, had dropped him, mostly they ignored this side of him and treated him as if he were the same old Bill. He had no interest in women, long ago he had decided to remain celibate and had even stopped eating meat for a while. He was strict when he was younger, the passions caught him then, but now as he grew older he slowed down and cooled down simultaneously. His appetites had sloughed off him effortlessly, a fact he would not have believed at twenty.

His isolation remained, as he drifted away from 'ordinary people', he listened to their talk but found their lives faintly repellent, lacking compassion for the things that troubled them. They depressed him, too; everything seemed so small, petty and mean.

Not that his life was any grander but he knew about its emptiness; they didn't, or at least would not admit to it.

When the variety work dried up he started doing magic shows for kids, privately and in the parks in the summer. It was okay at first, but then he started to lose it, drop things, his jokes were too old-fashioned, the kids started to turn on him. He'd got his pension, but it didn't go very far. He liked a flutter from time to time but his luck hadn't been so good. He'd got into money problems of the pressing kind and the only thing he could do was to rent the flat out for three months to a bunch of students. They'd paid cash and lots of it, so he settled the debts and had enough to scrape by living on food handouts and the meals his friends bought. He had been scared but also excited at the thought of sleeping out; he only wished it were summer and he could bed down in a park.

At first it had been a terrible shock, living rough; he missed being able to shut the door. On the street you were always visible. Although people didn't look you in the eye, they watched. There was no privacy, but at the same time other people pretended not to see you. He grew a thicker skin, became less fastidious, more aggressive and began talking to himself. His clothes grew dirtier, he lost his suitcase early on and was reduced to sorting through piles of cast-offs in secondhand shops.

The first night he went to a hostel, or rather joined the queue, but was turned away; it was full. He wandered down the South Bank and fell in with an Irishman who showed him the tunnels. They both bedded down there, freezing, drunk. In the morning he felt chipper and they had eaten breakfast in a caff in Waterloo opposite a building site. It was there he'd found the wardrobe. He bought his friend half a bottle of cider and they carried the thing to his patch in the tunnels. Lying on the wardrobe meant he didn't get the cold damp of the river from lying on the concrete. But his health deteriorated rapidly, he lost weight and his bones ached most of the time. He was developing a deep heaving cough which produced thick green phlegm.

His body was suffering but paradoxically he'd never felt better. Life was simple, honed down to the bare necessities; eating, washing, keeping warm, passing the time of day with people he met. Keeping clean was the hardest, it was so cold he wore all his warm clothes at once, layer upon layer. He had a bath twice a week at the public baths in the Borough and changed into clean clothes, thin, summer ones. Then he went to the council laundry and washed the dirty ones and sat shivering until they dried. Sometimes he couldn't be bothered and bought clean ones from junk shops. He still stank of the streets, a kind of metallic, concrete, bacon smell that you got in old railway carriages. He was presentable enough to get into libraries to read the papers and to wander around the South Bank and listen to jazz in the foyer. The security guards watched him, but if he bought a cup of tea they let him be.

He didn't tell his regular friends and after a while stopped seeing them; he didn't want them to know he'd fallen on such hard times. His pride, and also a fierce guarding of his secret life; he felt like a boy again, footloose, free of responsibilities. Knowing he would go back to his flat altered things. It was a game for him; sometimes he felt guilty. People tried to persuade him to sell the street paper but he was too ashamed, afraid someone he knew might pass him in the street.

His time was nearly up, the students were leaving a week early and he felt sad and excited. Life in his flat, with the gas fire and a warm soft bed, seemed so appealing, but he knew that when he closed the door he would be alone in a way he hadn't been these last three months.

The train pulled into Bethnal Green. Bill collected himself and left the carriage. Outside, the narrow High Street was crowded with shoppers, women wheeling huge baskets of laundry, shuffling pensioners, lounging adolescents. He walked slowly, anticipating the silence of the temple. He was delighted when the Buddhists moved here, this was his old hunting ground; he still had family scattered around the estates to the back of it. They were English Buddhists who had built a temple in a small disused warehouse. The statue of Buddha was golden, about eight foot high. A sea of white candles swayed at his feet and incense was always burning, sweet Indian incense.

The temple was open like churches used to be. Bill slipped in and, putting his palms together, bowed low to the glittering statue. Today it was garlanded with turquoise and cerise paper flowers, it was a festival day. A faint light filtered from the high windows, the room was long and wide with bare varnished floorboards and magnolia walls. The air was calm, silent, pregnant. Bill took a mat and sat cross-legged in front of the smiling golden statue.

Closing his eyes he took several deep breaths, filling his lungs, holding the breath and slowly exhaling. He followed this rhythmic pranayama for several minutes until he felt his energy both sink and expand. He concentrated on a spot between his eyebrows and, focusing his energy there, allowed light to accumulate and then diffuse into his whole body, until it was filled with golden light. His breathing became shallow and his thoughts slow, he felt a familiar peacefulness. He asked for guidance, he wanted a debt to be paid, for justice to be done. He didn't want revenge but a reckoning.

He sat for a long time, in the warm reflected glow of the Buddha. Somewhere a cymbal sounded and the spell was lifted. Devotees silently filed in, taking their prayer mats and settled into morning prayers. Bill stayed sitting for a while to re-orient himself. He stood up stiffly and bent down in thanks before walking slowly out. A monk in saffron waited by the door; they exchanged smiles as they passed. The serenity of the place was sublime.

Bill walked around the corner to the café run by the women of the order and bought a bowl of thin vegetable and miso soup. He sat down at one of the pine tables, staring emptily while the soup cooled down. The café was empty, the women were busy preparing for the lunch. He sipped his soup slowly, savouring the pungent taste of miso, with cabbage and carrots, soul food. The stillness of the temple lingered. When he had finished, he sat back and smiled. He decided to go and see how the boy was doing.

Bill left the calm of the café and moved onto the bursting pavement. Avoiding screaming kids and women laden with shopping he walked purposefully toward the tube station.

Chapter Nineteen

'What happened to your friend, Alice? You know, Patricia was it? You used to hang around with her years ago. Did she die or what?'

Alice shifts uncomfortably in her chair. Not only is the flat falling to pieces but so is the furniture, she can feel a spring pressing against her thigh. The smoke of several joss sticks has banished the worst of the catty smell. But the place feels grimy, she is dubious of even the crockery. They have drunk a good deal of tea and finished off a packet of custard creams that Alice was going to take to the club. It is past her lunchtime and her tummy is rumbling. Now Elsie is asking about Pat, the last person she wants to talk about.

Pat had gone off the rails in a big way. Alice guessed she was not quite normal by the way she dressed, in rough shapeless men's clothes and her hair cropped. She looked, well, masculine. Alice had often wondered what came first, her looks or her tastes. Pat hung round a theatre Alice'd worked at, doing scene shifting or building and they'd struck up a casual friendship.

Pat was intense but not bright, she seemed to stumble over her feelings like she was a grown-up kid. Alice didn't realise Pat had a crush on her until one of the boys had made a joke about it. Alice was shocked rigid and for a while avoided her. But seeing her downcast face she decided it was all harmless enough and they resumed their outings of cream teas and gin and limes.

They had such fun together, taking the train down to Brighton for the day or rushing round the West End pubs giggling like schoolgirls. Alice hadn't noticed how much Pat was drinking, until it got serious. Pat started in the mornings and towards afternoon became alternately aggressive and weepy. The fun stopped and from then on there was a swift decline. One morning she found Pat with her hand in her purse. Pat had lost her job some time before, and they'd had a great row. She had stormed out and they had never spoken again. Alice saw her once very drunk walking along Shaftesbury Avenue and had hidden in a shop doorway rather than meet her. She supposed she was dead by now. It was all such a long time ago.

She didn't answer Elsie's question, nor would she. Nosey parker! 'You hungry, Elsie? I'm starving. How about some fish and chips as a treat?'

'Chips maybe. Do you want to go and get them?'

'Let's go together. You need some air – you haven't been out all day.'

Elsie watches her, she is a sly old fox that was certain. But why not a little stroll? It is true she is feeling better, it's the company. She spends too much time on her own, brooding. By now Elsie is up and dressed so she just pulls her coat on. 'Must get some cat food too while we're out.' She picks up her handbag awkwardly and the contents spill out on the carpet. A pile of notes flutter to the floor.

Alice gasps. 'Elsie, what are you doing with all this cash lying about? Why isn't it in the bank? You might get robbed!'

She bends over to help pick it up, counting it as she does. 'Elsie there's over three hundred quid here. Where did this money come from?'

'Oh, I won it on the horses,' Elsie lies. She sweats and panics about being found out. That is another thing she'll have to give up. It is all getting too much for her. She is an old lady, after all. Alice is watching her with her beady eye.

'Elsie!'

'Look, I can't tell you, okay? Let's go out before we argue.'

They button up their coats and put on warm hats and gloves. Outside they walk stiffly and slowly, arm in arm. The sun is trying to shine but there is a bitter February wind. Lunchtime at the primary school is announced by a roar and babble of tiny voices bursting from the playground. They both stop and watch the woollen bundles rushing backwards and forwards screaming, laughing, playing tag, skipping, chasing a football. Their bursting, shrieking, exuberant life force ricochets around the high walled playground. Elsie and Alice stand a while with their noses to the gate, watching. A gust of wind rattles their teeth and pulls at their hats. Bitterly cold, they move slowly on.

'God, I'd hate to be growing up now, wouldn't you, Elsie?'

'Was it so good in our day? No, it's better now. People were so closed when we were young. All that prejudice. It wasn't so safe neither, despite what they say. What about them blackshirts and the awful strike and the hunger? Bet kids aren't hungry like we were. No, they're luckier than we were. I'm not sentimental for back to backs and bread and dripping. No!'

'But there weren't kids sleeping rough and drugs. It wasn't so dangerous. You can hardly walk out alone these days, I never carry a handbag.'

'Thieving didn't just get invented, Alice. Old people with short memories pretend it was better, but it wasn't. Think of all that housework, mangles, steam irons, coal fires, no hoovers.'

'Well in your case, dear, I would have thought the presence of a hoover neither here nor there!' Hungry, Alice is getting ratty.

'I've not been well. Give us a break, Alice.'

They walk into the little row of shops which once were butcher, baker and fishmonger, but are now boutiques, fancy restaurants and silk underwear shops. The chippy remains, although the English family has long gone. The owner is Greek and fries a mean chip. Flash cars park cheek by jowl at the kerbside, the place is buzzing with young upwardly mobile wealth. Even the pubs have become brasseries and wine bars, all but one.

'Fancy a Guinness with your lunch, Elsie?' Alice is partial to a medicinal dose.

'Well, why not? Let's make a day of it.'

They walk into the pub which is humming with the lunchtime trade.

'Oh, it's too busy in here, Alice! Lets get them to take away.'

Taking a fiver out of her purse Alice pushes through the crowds. One thing about being old was that people were forgiving of rudeness. It is almost expected that one should be crotchety and impatient. The old are indulged something rotten. She has no intention of waiting her turn. A path opens up before her and she shouts, 'Young man! Young man! Two bottles of Guinness to take away when you are ready!'

The barman stops in his tracks with the unfamiliar voice. He smiles. Alice smiles coyly back. Putty in her hands! They always were. She turns to Elsie and raises an eyebrow.

Elsie, however, is preoccupied. Over in a corner of the bar she has seen the toff. At first she does not trust her own eyes. But it is him all right. Her heart flips dangerously and she wonders if she is going to faint. She has never seen him here before, it is as if everything is catching up with her at the same time. Her legs turn to jelly and she puts an arm out to steady herself. A young blond man catches her and half leads, half carries her to a nearby chair. She sits down shakily.

'Are you all right?'

''Course I'm not bloody all right! I had a funny turn. I might die any minute!'

He looks alarmed. 'Shall I call an ambulance?'

'No! Here comes Alice with my Guinness.'

Alice looks concerned. 'What's the matter, old girl?'

'I had a funny turn, all this noise, these people . . .'

Alice catches her looking in the direction of the toff. She remembers that Elsie used to faint whenever she wanted to avoid someone. 'Who is it?'

Elsie blanches.

'Elsie, either you tell me what is going on or I'm leaving you right here!' Her voice is firm.

'Alice take me home!'

'Not until you spill the beans! Who is it anyway?' She is straining to get a glimpse of him, the pub is so crowded and she is dwarfed.

The barman comes over. 'Is she all right?'

'Yes, just had a funny turn, but thanks for asking.'

'I'll call a taxi if you want.'

'That's very sweet of you, but I think we'll stay here until she perks up. A brandy, that'll do the trick.' Alice is determined not to leave the pub until she has seen who Elsie was avoiding.

'One of your old gentlemen friends, was it?'

'Yes, yes, that's it.' Elsie is grasping at straws.

'Hmm. Point him out to me.'

'Alice, I can't!'

The crowd of young men who have been blocking her view move off in a bunch and Alice sees him. She catches his eye. He does not look away but smiles a sepulchral smile.

'That's him! The toff . . .'

'Alice, leave it be! For God's sake!' Elsie hisses, her face flushed with fear and the brandy. Too late, he is getting up. But wait a minute, he is with a young lad! Elsie flips, her resolve has been growing, Alice is like a breath of sanity. He won't do it any more, not if she has anything to do with it. She rises to her feet and screams, 'Stop him! Stop him!' Then she feels a pain, awful, tight, like a fist squeezing the life out of her. She sees angels. Everything goes bright, then foamy, then a film like gossamer covers her eyes; she swears she hears music. It goes black. She sees a light a long long way away and then passes out.

Alice watches Elsie rise and point. She screams and then turns an awful colour, beetroot and then blue, the veins on her forehead stand out like spaghetti. She falls forward clutching her chest. Luckily the young man is there and he catches her writhing body. Several people help to lay her on the ground. She is blue, she is twitching.

The landlord comes out and suggests moving her to a back room so as not to upset his customers who are straining to see the corpse. Between them, the landlord, the barman and the young man manhandle Elsie into a dusty back parlour and lie her on a table top. She looks awful, she might have been dead already.

The barman and landlord leave sharpish and Alice stands looking at the young man. She is stunned.

'She's going to die! Oh, my God! She's going to die.'

'Yes, she might die.'

Alice turns angrily on the young man. '*Don't say that*. She's my oldest friend. I don't want her to die!'

'No, but she might nevertheless. You had better prepare yourself.'

'Thanks a bunch!'

The barman brings a brandy, compliments of the house and Elsie's hat and gloves.

'The ambulance, where's the ambulance? Are you sure you called it?'

'It'll be here. When, we don't know, but it'll be here! The cuts you see. My aunt waited a whole hour. She died before they got to her,' he adds laconically.

'I don't want her to die, ring them again please!'

'Won't make them come any faster. A cardiac team is coming.' He peers at Elsie. 'Sure she's not dead already? She looks very white.'

It is true. The blue has gone, except around her lips. Her face is chalky, lifeless.

'Oh . . .' Alice wails.

'Here, drink this, it'll calm you.'

'*I don't want calming! I want a bloody ambulance*!'

On cue the ambulance crew walks in and set about their work. Blowing and beating, and waving her arms about. A faint glimmer of colour returns to Elsie's cheeks.

'Is she alive, is she?'

'She's alive all right. It looks like an overdose.'

'Don't be daft, she had a heart attack.'

'We'll get her to hospital and give her a thorough check.'

Alice follows the stretcher out. The pub hushes as they bring her through. The man has gone, she notices.

Chapter Twenty

Uther and Alice sit on hard plastic chairs. A message beams up on a screen in front of them. 'The average waiting time is twenty-five minutes . . . the average waiting time is thirty minutes . . . thank you for not smoking . . .'

They look at it. Hospitals have changed beyond recognition.

'It's like waiting for the Northern Line.'

'Bloody stupid idea.'

A security guard, fat, blue, decked with gilt badges walks slowly by. He has an expression of suspicion and disdain.

'Or *Miami Vice*.'

'What happened to the Health Service?'

'The Tories happened.'

'Still, it looks more appealing.'

'I'd rather it were falling down and we didn't have to wait so bloody long.'

'Twenty-five minutes isn't a long time.'

'If you're dying it is.'

'Elsie's not dying . . . do you really think it was a drugs overdose?'

'How could it be? She doesn't even take panadol.'

'Are you sure? She might keep it secret.'

'Well, she did used to have a Chinaman friend. Maybe she smokes opium. No, I can't believe it. She's not well though, that I do know. She probably got some foul disease from the cats.'

'Cats?'

'She's got hundreds of them, swarming, stinking all over her room. Bet they carry diseases.'

'Is she the cat lady?'

'What do you mean?'

'There's an old lady who lives by Primrose Hill who has cats. She wanders about at night laughing to herself and . . . chewing her lips.'

'What?'

'Chewing her lips, like people do who've taken speed or coke . . .'

'What are they when they're at home?'

'Drugs.'

'Oh, my lord . . . you mean?'

'Well . . . we'll see what the doctor says.'

'Nah, she couldn't, not Elsie surely?'

'You never can tell.'

'True enough.' She turns to face him. 'I don't know who you are. You might be a sex maniac for all I know.'

'I am.' He grins at her.

Laughing, she pushes him. 'So who are you?'

'I'm Uther Pendragon, King of the Britons.'

Her eyes widen. 'Blimey, that's worse than a sex maniac. You're bonkers! So where's your horse then, and your sword, and . . .'

They are interrupted by the doctor.

'Are you with Elsie McAvoy?'

'We are, I'm Alice and this is King Arthur.'

The doctor, small, slim, Asian, smiles weakly. She looks very, very tired. 'We're taking her in for observation. I wanted to ask you if she was taking any . . . medication.'

'My friend here seems to think she's a dope fiend. I have my doubts.'

The doctor looks at Uther. 'What kind of drugs?'

'I don't know for sure. I've just seen her wandering around where I live, talking to herself late at night, pulling at her hair and chewing her lips.'

'You're not related then?'

'No, we're friends.'

'Does she have family?'

'Dead, dear, all dead. I'm her oldest friend, my name's Alice, we were showgirls together, played the Palladium once we did.' She smiles again. 'You look tired dear, maybe you should have a sit down?'

'I am tired, I've been up for two nights.'

'Got a baby, have you?'

'A baby?' The doctor looks baffled. 'No, working.'

'And they don't give you rests, it's disgusting. You might fall asleep doing an operation or something.'

The doctor looks up nervously at the security guard who has stopped to listen.

'Ask at reception for which ward she'll be in, you can visit her at any time.'

'Thank you, dear, she will be all right, won't she?'

But the doctor has gone.

'Well!'

At reception they are told that she is sedated and won't wake until tomorrow. Her condition is stable.

'God! It's like getting blood out of a stone. I want to know if she is going to live!'

'*Yes!*' screams the receptionist. All the lights on her switchboard seem to be blinking. The security guard hovers.

'Perhaps you should answer some of those phones, dear!' says Alice. 'They might be important.'

Alice and Uther walk out of the hospital together and wander down the hill to South End Green.

'Horrible places!'

'I know. They make you feel ill just visiting.'

'Poor old Elsie.'

'Miss McAvoy to you! If I find she's been taking drugs I'll give her what for! At her age. Mind you, she's a close one, always has been. You never know with her what she's thinking. I thought she'd have calmed down at her age. My, my, a dope fiend! You wait till I tell them at the club!'

Alice has recovered from the shock and feels quite perky. Even her appetite has returned.

'You hungry? I didn't have lunch.'

'Oh, what a good idea. But not another pub.'

They find a nice restaurant. Waitresses in black with little aprons, like they used to have. They sit by the window so as to watch Hampstead's comings and goings. The food comes quickly and is passable. Alice has steak and kidney pie, to keep her strength up and Uther has roast beef. Followed by apple pie and ice cream and weak milky coffee. A treat.

When they have finished they both feel drowsy but nicely rounded. Neither wants to move but to drop off right there. But the place is closing for the evening. Reluctantly they pay and walk to the bus stop. An early darkness is falling. Grey daylight dripping into dusk. The day is finished. An icy rain slashes down and they huddle together. The bus shelter has been vandalised so the wind whips around them, concentrated by the holes where the glass had once been.

She stands close to him; he is big and solid and makes a good windbreak.

'You're not really King Arthur are you? Come on!'

'I am, but if you don't want to believe me, it's okay. I can afford to be generous with my subjects.'

'Generous, is it? Well then, you can generously pay this cab!'

She hails a cab which screeches to a halt.

Chapter Twenty-One

(

He stands scowling in the corner of the tube carriage. Life is a bloody bitch that is for sure! Just his luck! He still holds the ring. He looks at it again: it is eighteen carat, worth a few bob. He thinks about trying to sell it, but as he turns it around in his fingers another idea begins to form. It might be worth a deal more to its owner, seeing as how it was taken at the scene of the crime. Especially if its owner is a nob and didn't want it known what he got up to in his spare time. It might be worth a packet, more than he'd be paid for doing a risky run. He thinks, maybe the cabby did him a favour after all. Perhaps he'll go back to the flat and have a talk with the boy and try and find out where he could find the geezer. He'd apply pressure and get a nice lump sum, enough to settle him in Marbella.

He smiles to himself. Clever, that's what he is. He'll get what he wants, and with a lot less aggravation. He sits down and gazes benevolently at his reflection as the train speeds northwards.

Bill and Candida sit at the kitchen table eating chocolate cake and drinking tea. More tea! Candida thinks she'll drown in tea if the day lasts any longer. Bill is silent. He seems exhausted and she wonders if she should offer him a bed as well. But she feels self-conscious and keeps quiet. Mark is still sleeping. A real sleep this time, open-mouthed, arms outstretched, snoring gustily. She feels benign as she puts her head around the door to check on him. He has not undressed though, he doesn't feel that safe.

Bill still has no clear idea what to do. He is waiting for a sign. Meanwhile he feels in limbo. He watches the girl watching him. It is growing dark. She is still, he wonders what she is into. His street confidence evaporates inside four walls; he feels stunned by the day's events. The boy's life has burst into his ordered, lonely world. Everything has a meaning; such a cataclysmic happening must have awesome results. But what? He is waiting, flinching in anticipation of the next blow. Even that doesn't feel right, something is going to happen but he doesn't know what. It makes him feel tired, he is too old to withstand strong shocks. But he is also excited, he doesn't want to just go back to the same old life. He looks at Candida warily. Young women are troublesome. You have to be very careful how you treat them.

'I'm not keeping you from doing anything?'

'No. We'll just have to sit it out.'

'Yes, I'm afraid you're right.'

Candida watches the strange old man. He smells bad. She's dabbed some sandalwood on her wrist and is surreptitiously smelling it to keep the smell away. She can hardly believe it is the same jaunty man she met a few days ago. She is tired, she wishes he would go, but it is cold out there; she doesn't have the heart to say anything.

'More cake? Tea?'

'No thanks.'

They sit, waiting for time to pass, for the boy to wake up, for the others to come around. Bill wants to have a bath but is too embarrassed to ask. They sit on in silence.

In the taxi, Alice remembers the cats. She had the foresight to take Elsie's front door key and her purse. She leans forward and tells the cabby to drop her off: she'll go and have a good old clean. The cab pulls up outside Elsie's house, she leaves lionheart or whatever he calls himself, to pay.

The Hammer Horrors are in a gaggle in the hallway: they are bringing their equipment downstairs. Huge speakers, black and peeling, clutter up the space, and guitars in cases plastered with labels rest against the wall. There are several of them, they seem to be interchangeable. Dressed all in black, with pointy shoes and bird's nest hair, most have either khol or dark rings under their eyes, some have both. They wear a great deal of gothic jewellery: skulls with ruby eyes, snakes twisted on daggers, eagles in flight. They mumble as Alice greets them. She can't tell them apart, or which are men and which girls.

Alice takes a deep breath, 'Er, I'm a friend of Elsie,' she announces. They look downwards through their fringes and shuffle a bit more.

'Which one of you was it who borrowed the milk this morning?'

'That was Pete, he's upstairs,' a shaggy fuzzy man replies.

'Do you all live here?'

'Yea.' He offers himself as spokesman.

'Elsie . . .'

'Who?'

'She's the old lady who lives here. Alice points to her door.

'Oh, the cat lady!'

'Yes.'

'Those cats don't half niff.'

'Yea.'

'Yea.'

'I mean it's good, that she saves them like, but they're too many and they shit all over our plants.'

'Yea, last year, they ate the lot. We put them out the back to catch a bit of sun like, and next day they'd eaten the bloody lot.'

Alice is fast acquiring knowledge she has no wish to possess. She shakes her head vigorously as if to detach these thoughts. 'That is as maybe . . .'

'She's okay, isn't she? Pete told us she tried to, er . . . score from him.'

'What?'

'You know.'

'I *don't know*!'

Pete comes ambling down the dusty stairs. She does recognise him. He grins at her; his teeth need cleaning.

'Can you tell me what's going on in this house?'

'You're the bloke with the bus, aren't you?'

'Yeah, Uther.'

'Pete.'

'You play, don't you?'

'Yeah.'

'*Excuse me*!' Alice does not like being ignored.

'She's a coke head,' Pete says dully. 'Don't touch the stuff myself, makes my teeth ache.'

Alice turns and looks at Uther who says, 'Elsie is in hospital, she collapsed in the pub.'

'Drunk?'

'*No*!'

'No, they reckoned she'd OD'd.'

'Blimey, I knew she was overdoing it. Deals on wheels was here twice last week. Nasty piece of work he is. Don't know where she gets the money, she didn't look too good.'

'I want to sit down.'

Alice suddenly feels tired, it is all too much. She pushes her way through and fumbles for the key. Tears spring into her eyes. She is too old for all this. She wants to sit down and have a good old cry. Uther takes Elsie's key from her and opens the door. Aroma of cat fills the hallway. They all look at one another. Alice closes the door.

'Not today, Josephine, I can't face it.'

'Don't worry, we'll look after them.' A small, pink-haired girl speaks. She is grey and greasy looking, very thin. Her clothes are full of strategic holes. She has a ring in her ear connected by a chain to a ring in her nose, she wears what looks like a dog collar around her neck. She smiles. 'The boys and I will take care of everything. Won't we boys?'

Alice hears the steel in her voice and smiles. It is as good as done.

'Thank you, dear. I really appreciate it. Now here's her purse and there's more money in her handbag inside if you need to buy cat food or anything. Uther here will help you.'

Uther smiles his special smile, he's found the girl after all!

Chapter Twenty-Two

Elsie is floating. She wakes up to find herself floating near the ceiling. She giggles. Down below she sees her bed screened by a blue curtain. There are several people clustered around her body. She sees herself, laid out limp, pale, greenish-white. A machine by her head is bleeping like crazy. Two figures in white coats are leaning over her. She floats higher and finds herself spinning fast, faster, whizzing around and down, or is it up? She travels as though tunnelling into the earth's core, except it is space she is travelling through. She can see stars or the Milky Way. There is a bright light far, far off in the distance which rushes towards her. Bright, it dazzles but is welcoming and draws her forwards. She thinks she hears music, but not like any music she has ever heard, high and light, celestial really. It is very, very beautiful. Effortlessly, she moves towards the radiating light. Suddenly she is there.

Bathed in a primrose greenish blaze, she sees she is in a meadow. It is warm and summery. Fluffy white flowers are scattered in the long grass, while buttercups and meadowsweet mass around her feet. She is barefoot. A hazy sunshine falls upon her face, there is a light breeze playing with her hair and tugging at the edges of her robe. She feels at peace, radiant. She sees someone walking towards her, a great golden aura of light around him. His face is blackened in shadow. As he moves nearer, he seems to be gliding rather than walking. He opens his arms out wide into a welcome.

As he comes nearer his features emerge from the shadows. He looks like the Chinaman but is different somehow, taller, older. He has a long pony-tail and a little mandarin hat, with a moustache which reaches to his chest. He is wearing a red and gold brocade robe and felt slippers on his feet – they are black and have red dragons stitched on them. He bows to her and smiles, gesturing her to follow him. They move on air and slide from the meadow into the most exotic garden, it is Japanese and Grecian and Persian and all the gardens of the world mixed together. It is dazzling. All of the colours of the rainbow are blended and woven together, and some she has never seen, it is dazzling. Water tinkles and melds with a flute, she is sure she hears singing. She sees a fountain, a gazebo, a lot of white marble statues and floaty gossamer.

They sit down beside the fountain, and she listens to the gurgling, humming water. It is crystal, glittering, pure and cool. She dips her hand in the water; golden fish swim to and fro in the sparkling water, nibbling her fingers.

The Chinaman smiles and looks over her shoulders. She turns around. In the distance she is sure she can see her mum and her dead Auntie Flo, and isn't that Billy who died in the War? There is Mrs Snape whose house got bombed, and her schoolfriend Alfie who died of asthma. A whole life bursts up before her, as she recognises people she knew years and years ago.

One face watches without smiling. It is a thin boy with a bruised face; his eyes burn her. She remembers with a shock he is one of the boys she found for the toff. The boy passes by. Another crowd of faces emerge from the shadow, they smile at her but shake their heads. She turns back to the Chinaman. He takes one of her hands and he, too, shakes his head, smiling. He stands up and pushes her gently backwards. She falls reeling, spinning, tossing back into the darkness. Opening her eyes she sees the blue curtains and knows at once that the bastards have sent her back.

A crowd of people are staring at her, stethoscopes draped across their shoulders like expensive furs. She looks at them sullenly.

'Well, Mrs McAvoy we nearly lost you then!' A bespectacled man leans over her. He is thin, young, well-scrubbed with a plummy accent. The last thing she needs to see, having been kicked out of paradise. A bilious rage seeps out.

'Up yer bum!'

'Now then . . .'

'Sod off, will you!'

Someone titters.

'I understand we have a bit of a . . . ahem . . . drug problem, Mrs McAvoy.'

'*Do we*?'

She turns her face to the pillow and lets out a large fart. They move off awkwardly, clinking and rattling.

A few minutes later a nurse puts her head around the curtain. 'Well, I don't know! Farting at his nibs! You had us all in fits in the staff room. Don't you go doing it again, mind, or they'll be putting you in a locked ward. Made my day, though. Pompous old git he is.' She grins conspiratorially.

Elsie sits up. 'Any chance of a cup of tea? I'm parched!'

Dying has done her good, she feels like a new woman.

'The trolley be coming round in about five minutes. You're a caution you! Drugs at your age!'

Elsie's face falls. 'Oh.'

'Oh yes, we all know, me dear. They're sending you a counsellor round to really scramble your brain!' She laughs and disappears.

Elsie's euphoria leaves her. She wonders what will happen next. Will they lock her up? Send her to a home? She feels ashamed. But she remembers the garden and drags that memory back. That would be what she would think about, from now on.

Beautiful it was and so peaceful. Another head pops around the curtain, black, female with a wicked grin.

'Want your tea then, dearie?'

'Tea, I'd kill for a cup. Get me two will you and extra biscuits.'

The face laughs and disappears. Returning with two cups and a plate of biscuits she sits down on the bed. 'Did you really fart at the old bastard? Ha! Made my day it did. You want anything just ask for Marcia and I'll see you right.'

'Do you believe in heaven, Marcia?'

'Oh yes, the land of milk and honey.'

'I just floated up and went to this incredible place.'

'Did you now?' Marcia bites into one of the bourbons.

'Yes, I met the Chinaman there and lots of people who've died. They waved to me.' She remembers the grey unsmiling face.

'. . . and the garden, it was beautiful. Do you think that was heaven?'

'Hmm, I don't know for sure, it could have been the Devil's trickery. He's everywhere, getting his long fingers into God's work. You have to keep a watch out, real vig-il-ent.' She stretches out the word to emphasise its importance.

'How would I know?'

'Oh the devil he leave tell-tale signs.' She winks conspiratorially. 'Whoops, here come de counsellor, prepare yoursel . . .' She winks, again and disappears.

'Good afternoon.' Elsie's eyes widen. She thought counsellors were grey-haired old women in tweeds with wire spectacles. He is ebony, tall, slim, drop-dead gorgeous and about forty years younger than her.

'Hello.' She smiles but remembers her falsies have been taken out and snaps her mouth shut.

'May I sit down?' He sits without waiting.

'Now then . . .' he begins. She is transfixed, he is so beautiful. 'I understand you have been using . . .'

'It's okay I've given up. I've learned my lesson.' Elsie thinks this is what's required.

'What lesson might that be?'

'Er, I'm too old, my heart's too weak.'

'Ah . . .' He looks unconvinced. 'Well . . .'

'It's the pain you see . . .'

'The pain?'

'Yes, that's why I started. I smoked it for years . . .'

'Smoked it?'

'Opium, but then the Chinaman died and I needed something else, so I got hold of this stuff. But it's too strong. Opium suited me . . . er . . .'

'Ah . . .'

'Better . . can't get that on prescription.'

'I'm afraid not.'

'Will you tell anyone?'

'It will go on your notes, but the police won't be told. I would be careful in future if I were you.'

'Careful?'

'That you don't have a visit from the drug squad, they have a way of finding these things out.'

'Oh, my God!'

'Tell me about the pain . . .'

'Years ago, oh you don't want to hear all this . . .'

'Go on.'

'I was, oh seventeen . . . ' she tells him. Quickly, speaking softly, dry-eyed, she tells him of her brief affair with the airman and how, finding herself pregnant, realised he wouldn't acknowledge the child as his. He said if she had slept with him, then who else had she screwed. She sat it out and went alone to the Mother and Baby hospital in Clapton, and suffered the sneering contempt of the nuns. No one called her a tart, they didn't need to. Hatchet-faced women from the adoption agency visited her, gave her the paper to sign. Labour lasted three days, as if neither of them wanted to part. In the end they ripped her daughter out with forceps and left her legs wide open. She stretched her arms out for the baby but the nurse said best not. She wailed, she at least wanted to see her, and was shown the prune face, wrapped in a hospital blanket. Their eyes met and she whispered, 'Sorry, sorry,' before her baby girl was taken away for ever.

Sewn up, she'd drunk sage tea to dry up the milk and gone back to work. Outside she appeared the same, but inside she rolled a boulder across her heart. No one knew. She kept it as a bitter secret. Never again did she let herself go. Her heart walled in didn't let its guard down. Her steely resolve kept her going, nursed her corrosive hatred of men who could just walk lightly away, the nice orderly types who judged without compassion or humanity. She hated them all.

Fifty years on the hatred, like acid, had burned deep and she was as callous as those women had been all those years ago. Her eyes were cold, she took care of herself and no one else, except her pussies, and she was under no illusions about their loyalties. She doesn't say all this, but deals out her story in a flat monotone voice.

When she is finished Elsie sits back against the pillows her face set hard. She feels the bile rising, her bitterness is palpable. She keeps seeing a face float before her, the young man, from her dream. The counsellor sits impassive, he is looking at his watch.

'It won't make the pain better.'

'It does, for a time at least. It's all I have.'

'I don't believe that.'

Elsie feels a volcano tremble inside her, tears spring like fountains out of her screwed up eyes. Her chest heaves with dry, rasping sobs. She bends forward and leans her forehead on his proffered shoulder, howling. Suddenly the tears stop, the door clangs shut. She lifts her head and lies back, eyes closed on the pillow.

'I'm tired.'

'I'll come back tomorrow.'

'If you want.'

He leaves silently and she drifts off into an exhausted sleep, sleeping heavily, dreamlessly, for the rest of the day and through the night.

Chapter Twenty-Three

☾

Uther takes Alice back to his bus. He decides she needs a cup of tea and a slice of cake. Alice goes along with him mutely, passively, in a state of shock. Her world has been built on shifting sands and a wave has swept it all into the sea. It is all rotten, fragile, temporary. Going into a bright blue bus is just another of the bizarre things that are happening to her.

Uther sits her down and puts the kettle on to boil. He stands with his back to her staring out of the window. He goes to look for his ephemeris to see what the planets are doing. He finds the page and sees it was an eclipse yesterday, in Pisces. No wonder there is chaos, confusion, weird happenings with drugs, not to mention the rain. It is pelting down, splotches of grey London water stuck to the windows, trailing lazily down the glass. He can see puddles gathering on the darkened pavement, glistening with the reflected yellow street light.

Eclipses are bad omens, the light of the sun blotted out both figuratively and symbolically. For him it is the promise of a mysterious woman. Neptune, ruler of Pisces the illusionist, dissolver, glamour queen. She is that all right, no wonder he'd fallen for her. But she is a fantasy, he doesn't know if he'll see her again. She hadn't told him where she lived. He is bewitched, he is thinking about her too much, needs to shake her off.

'A penny for them.'

'Ah, I was thinking about a lady.'

'Does she love you?'

'I don't know, I've only just met her. We had a row.'

'Oh dear, serious was it?'

'I hope not, but I don't know where she lives, or her phone number.'

'Well, she'll find you, in this great thing. Why don't you live in a house like normal people?'

'Guess I'm not normal.'

Alice regards him. 'No, I guess someone who thinks he's King Arthur can't be that normal. Where you from then?'

'Cornwall.'

'Of course, goes without saying. Why do you think Elsie took drugs? What would she do such a thing like that for?'

'To escape, that's the usual reason, or boredom, of course. Heavy drugs like coke though, usually for excitement, dancing, clubs . . .'

'But what would she be doing with such a thing? I don't understand it. Do you take them?'

'Not coke, it's too harsh, but grass, yes, of course. Everyone does, don't they?'

'Grass, what's that?'

'Marijuana, pot . . .'

'You got some?'

'Er, yes . . .'

'Let me have a look.' And seeing his doubtful face she says, 'Go on. I'm trying to understand something.'

Reluctantly he finds the pouch and sprinkles some out on the table top. Alice looks closely, smells it, then pops a bit in her mouth. She chews it carefully.

'Tastes like, um, sage, some herb.'

'Marijuana.'

He sweeps it into a pile, he could do with a joint right now, just to mellow out. Their eyes meet.

'So how do you take it?'

'You smoke it.'

'In a cigarette?'

'Or you can make cakes or cookies with it or tea . . .'

'Well, better than PG Tips, eh!'

'Listen, I don't think this is such a great idea . . .' '

'Well, how strong is it? Stronger than gin?'

'No, very different. Makes you feel very different but not out of control like alcohol.'

'Is it nice?'

'Yea, you giggle a lot and get the munchies, for chocolate, sweet things.'

'Go on, make some tea.'

The giggles can be heard on the other side of the street. They eat the remains of the cake and a packet of chocolate biscuits.

Alice sends him out to forage for more and he comes back with handfuls of sweets, a bottle of lemonade and crisps and peanuts. They wolf them down. By now Uther is singing Cornish ballads and Alice is showing him what her still shapely legs can do up and down the aisle of the bus.

Eventually they come down, the energy drained out of them. Uther walks Alice home through the empty, rained-on streets. Although it is not late the heavy rain and fierce cold has driven most people inside. Alice lives across the High Street under the railway bridge and in a side road to the right. It is a low-level council block, clean, well-maintained, square-bricked building.

Mostly old people live there. Alice is on nodding acquaintance with all her neighbours and chats with several of them when they meet on the stairs or in the street. A quiet, respectable residential street. She'd fought tooth and nail to get her place and like the other residents had banded together to make sure standards were maintained. Buildings went downhill very quickly unless you were careful. Before you knew it there would be junkies and prostitutes and vandals all over the place, not to mention muggings and robbings and worse.

It all looks different now. In the glittering night air the beads of moisture are held almost transparent in the frosted mist. Alice feels daunted at the prospect of going home alone. She's had so much company today she dreads the lonely place. Boxed in by straight walls, flat glass emptiness.

'Come in, will you?' She looks at him hopefully.

'Of course, just to see you settled.' Uther feels a warmth from her he'd never found in his mother. She is still and friendly and open, his mother is altogether too bony and angular. He decides the flats don't suit Alice, the place has a death-like feel, as though ghosts live there. This would be a prison to live in. He wonders if the residents see him now whether they will let him past the front hall.

She leads him through the entrance. A potted plant, which on second glance turns out to be plastic, dominates the square linoleum floor. A mawkish picture of puppies and a baby with a huge glistening tear is found on one of the salmon coloured walls. They make silent progress along the carpeted corridor and then press the button for the lift. He realises just how stoned he is, the trouble with tea is it has a way of zapping you from behind. Alice looks bemused, her hat set at an eccentric angle. They grin conspiratorially.

The lift arrives noiselessly and draws them up one floor. They step out into a similar world, turquoise rather than salmon. Silent. Alice opens the door in front of the lift painted a tasteful mushroom and they go in.

Uther gasps; he has not been prepared. Alice is evidently an aficionado of pink. The whole flat has a pink frilly, fluffy ruched air. The carpet is pink, the sofa as well, shiny satin, there are raspberry velvet curtains pink and cream striped satin wallpaper, he feels sick looking at it. Porcelain ornaments clutter the surfaces, china dogs, vases, figurines. Soft-focused mass market prints are tastefully hung around the room. Perhaps his original evaluation has been wrong, Alice seems to fit in perfectly.

He follows her into the kitchen, bright with fluorescent light and blinks owl-like. He wants to run. He feels the cloying saccharine tentacles of working-class respectability. It makes his hair stand on end. Alice is busily brewing a pot of tea. Uther starts to sneeze, he always does when he feels trapped. He looks out of the window into the darkened street.

It is a a typical North London street, on this side neat sixties council blocks, on the other a row of crumbling four-storey Victorian houses. High steps chipped and rubbish strewn, leading to large bay windows and a scabby patch of greenery in the front boasting a motley collection of dustbins. The windows have curtains, albeit poor quality, so he guesses they are not squats, private landlords perhaps.

As he watches, the front door opens and an old man comes slowly out. He is tall and thin, and walks with a slight stoop slowly down the steps made slippery by the rain; there is no hand rail. He pulls his coat collar up as the slashing rain pounds on his bare head. He seems a sad, vulnerable old man. Alice comes up beside him to see what he is looking at. 'That's Bill, one of Elsie's friends! I must tell him she's in hospital.' Dragging Uther and picking up her bag, they both leave the flat.

Alice directs him to run, she will catch him up. Uther runs from the sugared prison of the flat. He finds the stairs and takes them two at a time. A taxi has drawn up outside the house and the old man is talking animatedly to the driver. Uther can't see properly, he is waiting to cross the road, a driver, obviously lost, dawdles frustratingly.

Finally Uther crosses. The taxi is still there, he feels bashful, now, unsure, he holds back. The old man is arguing with the cabby, a woman. It appears she doesn't want to do something. Another man arrives, small, hard looking, and he joins in.

The three of them look up as Uther walks over. He explains he is a friend of Alice. When Bill looks blank he explains about Elsie. Bill voices concern as Alice arrives, puffing. She looks at the cabby and cries out and the two of them stand for a long frozen minute, looking at each other.

The three men watch them, the women are laughing and holding each other. Bill suggests they all go back upstairs and have a nice cup of tea. The two women follow the men up the long steps to Candida's flat.

Chapter Twenty-Four

Candida is still sitting at the kitchen table when the bell goes. It is Bill. He found some other people and is coming back. She is exhausted but has passed the stage of wanting sleep; she feels wiry, on edge, hyped. The crowd files in. Two women she doesn't know are deep in conversation, Bill has brought back the bloke and, to her delight, Uther. They run to each other and then stand back silently self-conscious. Then as there is so much hugging and babble around they gingerly put their arms around one another. The bloke watches but says nothing.

Bill is making tea, the bloke picking at the chocolate cake, while the two women have wandered off into the living room. Candida follows them and turns on the lamps, the fire is roaring, the room is hot and airless. She sinks down on some cushions and Uther sits close beside her. Bill comes in with the tea and the bloke with a plate of sliced bread and long-handled toasting forks. He and Bill set about toasting the bread, Uther butters and jams it and they all sit back eating the dripping doorsteps, strawberry seeds stuck in their teeth.

No one mentions the boy until his bedraggled ghost pushes his way into their minds. Pat tells Alice that Bill found the boy, explaining what happened to him. Bill says he has had no further ideas but thought he would go to the café later on to see if anyone remembers the boy and the man who picked him up. The bloke says he will go with him. But Pat is worried, she asks whether that is the important thing. To find those responsible. Was that what mattered, in any case, what would they do if they found him? Beat him up, adding violence to violence? Was that what the boy needed? Someone else to get beaten up on his behalf? Was revenge the only option, maybe he needed other things? Candida agrees, she thinks he needs looking after, healing, safety, hope. Uther disagrees. He says Bill is right, they need to find the people who attacked him and make sure they didn't hurt anyone else. Alice says bitterly that putting the bastards in prison will make. not make the boy's wounds heal faster and in fact will make no difference at all. He is a child and needs a loving home so that maybe he might grow up not feeling bitter.

'And what about the next kid and the next that these people get hold of?' Bill is adamant that something has to be done. But he does agree that the police are out of the question and as for doing more violence, he for one was far to old for that kind of business, not that he'd ever liked it much in any case. Uther suggests that maybe they could denounce the perpetrators publicly.

Candida says, 'Women in Australia tar and feather rapists and tie them to trees in public places with a sign around their necks.'

The men shudder and say isn't that a little drastic, going too far?

She says 'No, rape was "going too far",' and asks them how they would feel.

There is a short, uncomfortable silence and then they all speak together. The women say heal, the men want revenge. The three of them sit in a huddle and mutter, the women look away, each in their own thoughts. Alice and Pat get up to leave. They hold hands and say they are going to have a long talk. Alice leaves Candida her address and the name of the hospital where Elsie is.

Seeing Alice about to leave, Bill suggests they should all meet here again tomorrow at the same time. Pat says she will ask around to see if there is any more news. She promises to come back tomorrow and they leave together. Bill, Uther and the bloke are putting on their coats too, they are going to the café to talk to the people there. Candida is fearful for their safety, but knows they will go ahead whatever she says.

Shutting the door she leans on the sleek wood and hangs her head. She feels there is worse to come, meanwhile she has to sleep.

As she walks back into the living room she sees the boy, he must have been awake for some time and she wonders if he heard their arguments. He looks hardened somehow. She remembers the soft, childlike face sleeping but now she can see his gauntness, hollow eye sockets, bony jaw. His arms hang at his sides unnaturally as though he is keeping them down by sheer force of will. He is shaking, yet his jaw is clenched and the muscles bulge out behind the jawbone. His eyes are hard, black flints. She feels a flicker of fear and, as she registers it, he smiles a cold smile, but says nothing.

She is aware for the first time that she is alone with this man-child. He has lost the soft bruised look of the morning and it is as if those tender helpless feelings have crystallised into a darker threatening passion. She feels his steady gaze challenge her, but doesn't know whether to react to his violent stare or to ignore it. Her voice fails her. *In extremis* her childhood muteness returns. They stand eye to eye, grimly watching each other. She wants to smile but the muscles in her jaw are frozen shut; a trace of nausea worms its way up her throat.

The boy takes a step towards her. It breaks the spell. Walking stiffly she makes her way into the kitchen, the joints of her knees seem unbending, awkward. She fills the sink with hot water from the tap and, shaking like a jelly, tries to wash up. He is beside her silently, leaning over to see her face.

'Scared are you?' he jeers.

She glances back with hunted eyes and then looks down and, stamping her foot, turns to face him. 'Listen, if you want to go back to the gutter, to the tunnels, go back. *Go go go go go!*'

He smiles and moves away. 'I want something to eat.'

'Then cook it.'

'No, I want you to cook me something to eat.' She thinks about Alice across the road and wonders if he'll let her leave the flat.

'I don't have much, I'll have to go out . . .'

'No I don't want you to go out.' He starts to open the cupboards, taking out dried food, spaghetti, tins of beans, packets of lentils, chickpeas, sesame seeds, curry powder. 'Make something from all this.'

'I can't!'

He picks up a tin of spaghetti and throws it in her face. 'You will!'

She screams as it hits her cheekbone. The edge of the tin cuts the flesh and blood dribbles down her face. She is white with terror. All the blood seems to leave her body, her legs collapse and in slow motion she sinks to the ground. She closes her eyes and leans her head back against the oven door.

He watches her feeling little, numb. The flies were there when he woke, buzzing and buzzing inside his head. He is sure there are maggots, too, under his skin: his flesh crawls with their filth. He hits her. It pleases him, to see her crumpled on the floor. He watches to see what she will do next. Instinctively his eye wanders around the kitchen. A red-handled bread knife is lying on the table to his right. He takes it and slips it into the waistband of his trousers.

He hears a padding like a large dog behind him. He feels warm breath on his hand but when he looks down he sees nothing. He knows he is being watched, feels a prickle of fear, some nameless thing is pacing around him. He feels immobile, he cannot move, like a fly caught in a web. Something is weaving around his arms, his legs, his mouth; he feels wrapped and silent as though covered like a mummy in a cartoon. Only his black frightened eyes stare out over the unseen bandages. He begins to dissolve from the inside out, like sugar in warm water, and syrup spreads out in his veins and arteries. He lies sideways on the floor. He examines some pieces of bread and a nut which lies on the sticky lino. A ball of dust with long tendrils of red hair is crouched under the table. He becomes aware of the cold blade of the knife digging into the small of his back. A warm breath on his upper lip makes him look down, and he catches a glimpse of orange black like a cat's eye. He feels more afraid and begins to cry, piteously whimpering, tears falling down his cheeks and collecting in a small puddle by the side of his face. His breath comes in short sharp sobs and clings to his ribs.

Candida turns to look at him. Where the tin met her face a red mark has appeared, blood drips steadily onto her purple shirt. She looks back stunned, her lips pale, tearful. 'You bastard.'

She gets up heavily and walks around him, eases the bread knife out of his trousers and goes into the bathroom. Panic stricken that he will be left here, he calls out to her. She ignores him and he hears her running a bath. The door slams shut and the bolt slides closed.

He lies there, waves of foetid, corrosive despair crash his heart. He is worthless and useless and vile, just like they said. He is better off dead. He just needs to do it. He wishes they'd finished him off last night. An ending. He imagines slashes on his wrist, a rope around his neck, a speeding train, chopped neatly, splattered on the track, on the bridge weighted down, a high London bridge with stones in his pockets. Or gas, he looks at the cooker, head in gas, wild fumes like glue and the dark night. He stops, blackness is a sobering thought. The endless night, just nothing? Ah, he isn't so sure. What about hell? The angry slashing holds appeal as though bloodletting might release tension.

But hitting women is crap, he wishes he had stopped himself. She was okay. He will say he is sorry and he won't ever do it again. He likes the feeling when she looks at him full of fear and respect. Then she takes him seriously. That's what slapping did. Knock them about and they listened. But it was still crap. He won't be like his dad for anything. He wants to be softly loved, not to have her creeping about like his mum, terrified. Lying, always lying, to cover up. Making him feel it is his fault. Never sticking up for him in case she got it too, which she did anyway. Especially if he'd lost at the horses. He'd get it first, then her, then later squeaking bed springs. No wonder he'd never fancied women if they made you like that.

He felt revulsion at the thought of his mum's simpering, timid shuffle, of the plates of food which ended up smashed against the wall, the broken furniture. He'd get his dad for his mum then, they'd have each other. He knows this is crap, she'd find another dumb shit to take his dad's place.

She puts some rescue remedy in the bath, for shock and fear, and lots of lavender oil for the bruising. It isn't a deep cut but she bruises easily. Gently she rubs comfrey on to the bruise: it'll bring it out and clear it up quickly. Her heart is still racing, she forces herself to calm down and think clearly. The knife is on the bathroom floor, its red handle reminds her of blood. Christ! He could have stabbed her, killed her! She wishes she'd brought the phone in, she needs help.

He might flip again, and she didn't want to be watching her back wondering if a knife was going into her. The cat slides through the door and stands watching her. She smiles, it sits still, watching.

Slowly the lavender unravels her muscles. She feels a weariness. Slipping gently in the water, she jerks awake. The flat is silent. The cat slips out and wanders back into the kitchen. The boy is still lying on the floor but has turned on his belly. He is breathing steadily, short shallow breaths.

Candida steps quietly out of the bath and dries herself quickly. She'll make for her bedroom and barricade herself in until the men come back, let them deal with this. Slipping her dress over her steaming damp body she gently opens the door and tiptoes into her bedroom. Empty. She closes the door and pushes a large chest in front of it. Her heart rattles and she sits down dizzy from fear, exertion and the hot water.

The smell of the boy is on the sheets. She sprinkles some rosewater over them and climbs into the warm, soft bed. Soon she is sleeping, dreaming, restlessly muttering. Once she wakes sweating, her heart pounding, but there is nothing, no sound. The chest is still blocking the door and the cat sits watching her, his eye illuminated by the street light. She turns over and sleeps.

The boy lies on the floor. He doesn't sleep but listens to the sounds in the flat below and waits for the men to return. He wonders if he should just go and forget about all of them, but he waits for his punishment, almost content, knowing this is how the world works and this is his place in its workings.

Chapter Twenty-Five

☾

Candida is woken by a knocking on the door. Groggy, she takes some time to float back to consciousness. Her body is weighed down, pitted at chest level, it is only with great effort she opens her eyes. When she hears his voice, the desire to drift off and forget everything is too strong; sleep pulls at her, but his voice is persistent, whining, it burrows away in her cloudy mind until the irritation drags her back.

He calls her name and says he wants to talk. It strikes her how little she wants to speak to him, deal with his problems, she vaguely wonders why the men haven't returned. Defeated, she calls out testily, asking what he wants. He replies nervously that he has some tea for her, he is lonely, and cold, and wants to know how to get the fire going.

She wonders if it is safe; if he has returned to his other self, the vulnerable man-child. Reluctantly she gets up and sits down beside the door. She decides not to open it just yet. But the thought of tea is appealing.

'Why should I open my door to someone who hit me? I don't like you or want you here, not while I'm alone. You're dangerous.'

Silence.

'Look, violence I won't have, not in my house.' She gets up to look at her face. A small bruise, greenish yellow, has formed under her eye. Pressing the flesh, she winces; it is painful and swollen. The cut is small, the dried blood has rubbed off while she was sleeping.

'You'll be pleased to know I've got a black eye.'

'I'm sorry.'

'What use is that? "I'm sorry",' she mimics back. 'No use, that's what.'

'I'm better now, I had a funny turn. Your tea's getting cold. Please come out. I promise not to do it again.'

'Promise?'

'Promise, cross my heart . . .'

She drags the chest from behind the door and opens it. He is standing holding a pale mug of tea, tea leaves smeared down one side. He looks up pleadingly.

'Please . . . I am sorry.'

They walk together to the sitting room and she pokes around at the embers. A red brightness is revealed under the thick, white ash. She lays some kindling on top of the glowing fragments and scatters small pieces of coal on top of it. It is cold in the room; her breath mists on the glass as she draws the curtains. A faint daylight is visible. The rain is still falling and a solitary street light glows on. Looking across the road she wonders where Alice lives and guesses it will be the block of flats with the trim lawns and bad-tempered old men who shoo away playing children.

A large plane tree, its black dripping branches hanging across the window pane, shudders in a strong wind. Huddled figures under umbrellas scurry across the street and group miserably around a bus stop, as if it is a totem and they are waiting for deliverance.

She turns around to face the boy, who looks changed again, small, almost wrinkled, his fuzzy hair full of lint, his skin dull, lighter in patches. He looks away like a naughty child forced to stand still, his arms straight by his side, neck stretched sideways, examining the carpet. She walks up to him and he still looks away straining, his eyes misty with tears. One falls, she wipes it away with the sleeve of her jumper and puts her big fat arms around him and draws him into her. He shivers a little, thin and fragile under the borrowed clothes. Now tears run in torrents down his cheeks. She strokes his head, gently at first, then more firmly, rhythmically, and pulls his resisting body closer until his ribs press into her.

He wilts like a plant and she sits him down on the cushions and holds him. They sit a long time until the fire begins to fail and their shivering forces them to bank it. She puts the duvet around their shoulders; the yellow light of the flames is reflected in their faces.

'So? What happened?'

He looks away, ashamed. How to explain? He is afraid. He looks bleakly at the smoking fire.

'Talk!'

He stays silent. She watches his lower lip trembling again, with the awful need to run, run away. His heart pounds; all he sees is white panic.

'You changed so much, are you . . . have you . . .?' Candida doesn't know how to say: Are you crazy? Do you hear voices? Are you often violent? She waits and again the serpent of fear uncurls itself. She remembers the dog and asks herself if he would do that to a person, if he would do that to her. He brought badnesss with him. Maybe he is one of those people that disaster follows. Is he about to blight her life with pain, violence, bloodshed?

She curses herself for ending up alone with him; he could turn again at any minute. Her size might help her if it came to a hand to hand struggle, she could just lie on top of him. But he took the knife yesterday. Is she prepared to ward off a knife in the ribs? Is she able? Now he seems defenceless, but how long would that last? She wishes Bill would return and Uther . . . where are they? She stands up, letting her side of the duvet fall and paces across the room, crossing the threadbare carpet heavily.

On the table she sees the cards. Death, the grim reaper, bones and a huge scythe cutting down everyone; the bishop praying on his knees is helpless, death hears no supplications. Whose death? Hers? The boy is watching her fearfully. She looks out at the freezing day and feels it darkening but guesses it can't be so late. She sighs, his silence is making her fearful, she feels tired and does not want the responsibility. She wishes irritably that he would leave her alone and slink back to the tunnels and his bitter, mean life. The boy looks at her imploringly, he senses her exasperation and is afraid he will be thrown out in the streets. But if she tells him to go, he will, without any fuss, to show he is no animal. He has his pride, a small slice. He is fainting from hunger. He remembers the tin hitting her, and slumps further into himself.

She watches him dispassionately. He is so small and vulnerable. A paradox. Cruel thoughts unravel as she contemplates him. Perhaps after all she will throw him out, who cares, after all: one beggar, one rent boy more or less, so what? Maybe the rubbish heaps and tacky bars are where he belongs, and he is happier there than he ever might be here. What would Bill do with him, or Uther, for that matter? Doubtless they imagine she will look after him. She feels rebellious and cross. The assumptions men make! How dare they think she has no other work?

She takes up her cloak and announces she is going out, enough of this mothering. Before he can reply she has slammed the door and is striding down the stairs. A low fog has gathered and the air feels toxic, poisoned as though carbon monoxide lies suspended in the thick yellow mist. She coughs and bending her head deep into her coat makes her way across the road. She finds herself clutching the piece of paper Alice gave her.

Candida waits to cross the road, and waits. She remembers the road crossing lessons she was given as a child. Wait until the road was clear? Some time around four a.m. at best. The cars jam up her side of the road and she weaves her way through them, watching for cyclists and motorbikes. She finds herself in the middle when the start moving, traffic is passing by on both sides, the road is narrow, all it needs is for two lorries to come and she'll be squashed like a fly. She picks a likely looking car and smiles, he slows down letting her pass. Sometimes crossing the road is more than she can bear, she stays inside rather than run the gauntlet of frustrated, aggressive car drivers.

On the other side she looks up at the block of flats and then, curious, turns around. The boy's face is at the window, watching her. Irritated, she walks down the short driveway and presses the intercom. It crackles and a wavery voice answers. Is everyone afraid?

The boy watches her disappear into the building and lets the curtain go. He walks listlessly into the kitchen and begins to rummage around for food. He finds some eggs, crackers and cheese and sets about making a meal. He has watched his mum cook. He turns the gas up too high and the eggs burn at the bottom, but are still runny on top. He slices some cheese on them and mixes in some ketchup. He eats out of the pan, scooping the mixture with the crackers, which seem a bit soft. Finishing it off has just tickled his hunger, he looks for something more substantial. He finds a tin of spaghetti and heats that up with another egg stirred into it. The egg turns into filaments and then white and yellow lumps but he eats greedily; too quickly, it burns his mouth. He finishes the milk in the fridge and a packet of ginger biscuits.

Mark wanders around the flat picking things up, looking at them and throwing them down. He takes the beads from the lamp by her bedside and hangs them around his neck. He stands in front of the wardrobe and pulls out a white satin dress and holds it against his body. He poses in front of the long mirror and strokes the silky fabric. He pulls it on over his clothes and winds a glittery silver green scarf around his neck. He finds some lipsticks and eye shadows. He tries a deep orange lipgloss which makes his skin look paler, he wipes it off on the scarf and tries a crimson, then a plum, and finally settles for a peachy silver gloss. He finds some shimmery green eye shadow and spreads it over his eyes and then sets about cutting his hair. It isn't as easy as he imagines, the more he cuts the patchier it becomes. He throws down the scissors in disgust and tries on various earrings and settles for some that look like sherbet drops. He turns the cassette over and sets the music playing loudly. Spreading his arms wide he circles the room. Spinning slowly he weaves and dives and leaps and pirouettes, until beads of sweat stand up on his forehead. Suddenly, his energy leaves him. He lies on her bed and, pulling at the scarf around his neck, falls asleep.

Chapter Twenty-Six

Bill and Uther walk briskly side by side. They are both big men and have to dodge and weave on the narrow streets. They stop at a phone box and Bill rings the hospital. The voice says Elsie is recovering and visitors had best come tomorrow.

The bloke trails along behind them. Bill is relieved he came, he knows how to look after himself, his mean presence might come in handy. Uther is well-meaning, but soft and flabby, he'll probably run away or burst into tears at the first sign of trouble.

The rain is falling heavily and a stiff wind blows it against them. They walk with their heads down, hands in pockets. They cross into the tube station and descend the windy tunnels. It is late evening and the rush hour crush has passed. Two bleary drunks stagger in the northbound tunnel, grunting unintelligibly. A woman clutching a child and, trailing another, comes toward them. She grins a toothless smile and holds out a card saying she is a refugee and is hungry and will they give money. They pass her by. Eventually the train arrives and there is a surge of figures who have been waiting in the shadows. Everyone finds a seat and looks warily around.

The carriage holds a polyglot mixture of races, religions and even genders. A transvestite in a blonde wig, red six-inch high heels sits uneasily on the corner seat, she/he is made up extravagantly and wears a tight fitting lamé frock. Next to him are two Asian men with long beards and white caps, who sit quietly, watchful. Beside them sits an attractive young white man. His head is shaved in such a way that patterns, zigzags, wavy lines are contrasted with the pink flesh. He wears a thick gold earring and a red kerchief tied around his neck. He has wide trousers and expensive trainers. He sits, his legs outstretched, beating time with his fingers. Next to him are two overfed white men in cheap business suits. Heavy jowelled, pink-faced, their cheap brogues are worn down at the heel, the edges of a cardboard briefcase peeling its leather cover. They are talking loudly, boasting. One of them is eating a hamburger and the sweet smell of roasted flesh and onions fills the carriage. Two tourists sit wild-eyed on the edges of their seats wearing the ubiquitous blue jeans, white trainers, clutching small rucksacks. Blond, tanned man; tanned, well-manicured woman.

An empty can rolls along the wooden slatted floor, falling forwards as the train brakes and backwards as it accelerates. A newspaper has been stuffed between the seats, its edges flutter in the draft from the communicating doors. The train heaves and jerks into Euston, people pile in and struggle out. A traveller with a dog on a piece of string comes in with a thin girl behind him. They make their way down the carriages asking for spare change.

Most people sit seemingly oblivious but taut and ready for trouble from drunks and bores and flashers and beggars; suppressing the white fear of breaking down, of being stuck in a tunnel with this random section of humanity, the terror of claustrophobia. No one makes eye contact but watches alert, the air is electric with tension.

The bloke looks at his watch; eight o'clock. He wonders whether he should go to the meeting, he's brought his passport and a small bag, but decides the pickings will be richer following these two. Blackmail can go on for years and years, like life insurance or a pension. He smiles at the thought, the old cabby did him a favour, a real stroke of luck. He sits back, well pleased with himself.

At Tottenham Court Road they join the stream of people up the escalator and out into the bustle of the big intersection. Crowds of day trippers are getting out of their coaches to see a show at the Dominion, people hang around the phone boxes and the pizza stall, cars and taxis flash past in the drizzle, late shoppers and drunk office workers stand under umbrellas chatting, waiting for an empty cab.

Red buses thunder past heading north and east. They cross over and pass Centre Point.

Bill leads the way. The other two hang back, nervous; they have the usual heterosexual's fear of 'faggots', of seduction, contamination. They move closer together and walk into the bright warm den. It is pretty much empty, a couple are holding hands deep in conversation and glance up briefly. Uther barely suppresses a gasp. This is not his territory. The bloke begins to snarl and then remembers why he is here and manages an eery grin. Bill sits down and orders three beers from Ricardo.

They drink in silence, aware they are the outsiders. Ricardo sits on a stool on the other side of the counter. He is flicking through a paper languidly, keeping a sideways eye on the trio who've just entered. Clearly straight, maybe they are lost, but he guesses they are after something. Right enough the old man comes up to him.

'Excuse me.'

He watches Bill coolly, disdainfully, he can sweat for a change. 'Well?'

'I wonder if you could help me?'

The barman looks him up and down. 'I doubt it, dear.'

Bill smiles. He met lots of fairies in the theatre, they don't phase him. 'Listen, a friend of mine was in here last night.'

Their eyes meet. Ricardo knows immediately who it is and looks away. Damn the boy! Simple acts of kindness, he should have known better, knew it would cause trouble, and this he couldn't risk. 'So many people come in here, I can't remember faces.'

'Please try, he is only a kid.'

The waiter notices the present tense, and relaxes, so he hasn't ended up dead.

'What happened to him?'

Bill smiles. 'He's alive, but in a bad way.'

'Beaten up?'

'Yes . . . but . . .'

'Oh.' He understands. 'Poor kid.'

'He picked up the bloke here, a friend of mine drove the taxi.'

'I never saw the man before,' Ricardo lies.

Bill guesses he will lie, probably an illegal, doesn't need any trouble. 'Look, it's for the next one . . . he'll do it again, they'll do it again.'

'They? . . . oh God . . .' The barman sighs. 'He knew what he was doing, it wasn't as if it was the first time. He was a regular. I'd feed him and, more often than not, he'd leave with someone. I don't like it anymore than you do, but this kid knew what he was up to. He was surviving like me, like you.'

'And the man?'

'Strange grey eyes. About your age. No more. Go and don't come back! We can't afford trouble here.'

'I know, thanks anyway.' Bill pays for the beers and the three of them file out.

Bill wants to hang around just in case the man comes back, so they stand huddled under Centre Point and wait. A few people come in, the couple leave, but no sign of the man. After about an hour they are too cold to stand still any longer. They go back across the road to the theatre and buy some weak coffee in paper cups. Failure. Bill wonders if they should go on watching and waiting or if they are wasting their time. The man might never come back, and anyway would they recognise him if he did? Uther is all for going, he feels they have done what they could and that maybe the women were right. What good would it do even if they did find him? If they caught up with him he'd deny it, and who'd trust the word of the boy against a rich guy in a suit?

The bloke, hearing the description of the man, is eager to get rid of Bill and Uther. He says they should give in and accept they've done all they could. Bill remains obstinate; he wants that man just for five minutes, he wants to look into those sick eyes. But it is freezing. His bones ache with tiredness, he feels their luck has gone so he is persuaded by the other two.

Bill and Uther walk off to the bus stop in Tottenham Court Road and the bloke goes in the direction of Soho. After a hundred yards Bill stops and suggests that instead of going home they should have a drink. They turn into a tiny alleyway and he leads Uther into a dark pub with stained beams, worn leather seats and a profusion of horse brasses, amber glass and a real fire burning in the grate. The landlady greets Bill like a long lost friend and the two men stand by the fire until the ice melts from their veins. She brings them drinks and two plates of steaming pies, chips and peas. They sit down and eat in silence, feeling the heat and life return to them. They relax back in the deep leather corner chairs and Bill sips a whisky.

Uther is impressed, it is like a country pub in the middle of London; he feels like a character in Dickens. He watches Bill nod off and feels the whisky and the heavy suet pastry working on him too. He is woken by the landlady gently shaking him. Bill is snoring gustily. She brings them both a cup of strong dark coffee.

Bill wakes up very slowly. Uther asks her if they've been friends long. She laughs, showing her gold teeth and says Bill was like family, he married her cousin years back and she looked after him when his wife died. She is fond of Bill and thinks it would have made him happier if he'd married again. Uther finds it hard to imagine Bill married and says so. She says he's changed, become more distant, not colder but absent somehow. She knows he has a lady friend Primrose Hill way but has never met her.

Uther tells her about Elsie. She pushes Bill tenderly and teases him that she's heard all about his lady friend. Bill smiles and stretches like an old cat. He so wants a bed, clean sheets. He and Uther say goodbye at the door and Bill walks slowly and stiffly down towards the river.

Uther is too tired to think of any other thing except his bed. He hops on a bus and watches the passing cityscape dully as he makes his way northwards up Camden Road along the tatty High Street.

He cares little about the boy, it disgusts him, however hard he tries to be open-minded about it. The bloke is right when he said there were always other things one could do. He doesn't understand how the boy cares so little about his body to let strangers brutalise it. He loves sex but can't imagine doing it coldly, with strangers, for money. He always likes the women he beds, even if it doesn't last very long afterwards. Screwing someone you despised makes his flesh creep. He wishes the boy would go back to where he came from so he can take up with Candida again. He'll go and see her once the boy has gone. He doesn't like the way he looks at him, as though he was a phoney.

He is off his bus and about to cross the road when he sees the chick in the supermarket walking ahead of him. He'd forgotten about her. His pace quickens to catch her up. He calls out, she freezes, he says something reassuring and she turns and smiles.

He walks up to her, determined to be invited into her place; she'll make him feel better. They walk slowly past the shops; he feels the *frisson* of arousal; he moves closer to her, she doesn't move away. He is being charming and, charmed, she invites him in for a smoke.

They make their way chattering up into her place. Her father owns the flat and the lads, as she calls them, live with her. She is Jacqueline, an art student, at St Martin's. She is small, like Jane and very slender. She is wearing a long purple velvet coat, tight fitting, buttoned to the ground. She has on a black woollen hat with a bunch of plaster cherries on one side, out of which electric pink hair pokes out unevenly. She carries a plastic bag of food. He leans down to catch what she is saying; her eyes are green and her face pale, soft, very appealing. When she laughs she shows white, evenly spaced teeth. He likes her more and more.

They cross the road and walk up the battered steps of the house. Elsie's window is dark and her cats sit on the window sill, the dustbins and on the garden wall.

'How is the old lady?'

'The hospital says she's going to be okay, but it was an overdose, not a heart attack.'

'Oh.' She is guarded. Uther feels she doesn't want to talk about Elsie's drug habit, maybe she is involved.

'I've fed the cats.'

'Good.'

They climb the stairs to the first floor, she smells of sandalwood, delicious, he leans over her, lusting. She puts her key in the lock and stands back to let him in. The room is painted deep crimson red and has Indian wall hangings and low lights. There are cushions on the floor and a large sound system. The air is thick with smoke, joss sticks and joints slowly burn. There are about seven or eight people sitting or slumped on the floor, low music is playing, several guitars are balanced against the wall.

One man rises up to greet him and he recognises Pete from this morning. He sits down with him, takes a bottle of beer and a large, badly rolled joint. No one speaks. Jacqueline sits down beside Pete and leans her head across his knee while he strokes her hair absentmindedly. All the time she is watching Uther and smiling at him. He blushes with excitement. Pete must sense something.

She turns to Uther and tells him they have made a start on Elsie's room. But the place is in a right state. What she has done is to take the money out of there, throw all the cats out, with their bowls and the cat litter, and close the place up. She plans to find a couple of people and pay them to give it a thorough going over. She gets up and brings the handbag over and shows Uther its contents. He counts the money and looks at her. She looks coolly back, she stands with her back to her boyfriend and winks. There is a heavy silence. Uther stands up to leave, they look relieved, they walk him out to the top of the stairs.

'There is something strange happening, Jacqueline has seen lots of young boys, dossers most of them, coming and going. I can't understand it.'

Uther pales. 'Look I'm too tired now to think, let's talk in the morning . . .'

'We don't want any trouble.'

'I know, neither do I.' But I seem to be being dragged into this mess whatever I feel about it, he thinks. 'Why don't you come over to the bus. Breakfast tomorrow?'

'Okay.' Uther turns to say good night to Jacqueline and she blows him a kiss.

'Tomorrow, then.'

He turns and walks down the stairs. Outside he is met by a hundred flashing eyes, the cats are waiting, they wail and swarm around his legs, he kicks them out of the hallway and pushes his way through. One spits at him, he hears a hiss, several jump on the dustbin lids making a clatter, he turns quickly and half jogs along the road to his bus. He feels haunted by Elsie and her malevolent friend.

Chapter Twenty-Seven

Alice is bathing her eye. It doesn't need bathing but Candida needs some attention and so she sits still like an obedient child while hot water and TCP are dabbed on it. She is fascinated by Alice's flat. A kitsch paradise. Candida watches Alice fluttering around her face, chattering, smiling. She has good teeth. Candida watches, faintly repelled and wryly amused as Alice dances around her.

Alice tells her about dancing before the War; the chiffon and net dresses which gave way to austerity and finally to hardly any fun at all. She's been around and seen a thing or two, bucolic managers, love-sick stage door johnnies, the bitchiness of the girls and the drunken comics. She loved the glamour, but the work was hard, the pay lousy and if you weren't careful you'd be in the club and on your own.

She and Elsie had done one summer in Brighton, after the War. Bill was there too, he had taken them out for teas and gin and limes. He'd borrowed the stage manager's car and they'd driven to the Downs one glorious day. They sat at the top of Beachy Head and ate a picnic, drank Pims and port and lemon. They'd giggled between them which one would have Bill, they'd decided to share him and had teased him, then tried to kiss him and take his shirt off, but he was having none of it. Bill was embarrassed when they asked him if he was a virgin; he'd shrugged them off and threatened to throw them off the cliff if they didn't stop. He'd had a wife, but had kept her a secret, Alice didn't know why. Later she'd died and they'd stayed near him and stopped him drinking himself to death.

Candida feels tearful. Such long friendships, just how long had she known anyone? People don't like her much. She frightens them she thinks, or embarrasses them. People don't like long silences, strange lifestyles, illiteracy, fatness. She'd never had a real friend, only people who passed through and wanted something; food, a place to stay, an audience. Older people pitied her or were frustrated when she rejected their rescuing overtures. People of her own age took one look at her and drifted off, she was altogether too much. She sees no way out; she's hung around the edges of life for so long it seems normal. She tries imagining having a friend but can't.

She watches Alice, her face lit up with memories, gold-tipped, rose-coloured, fanciful. By now they were topping the bill at the Palladium or was it Hollywood? She isn't listening to the stories but watching the lights reflect in her eyes the sequins on her shoulders, the sound of forty tapping feet, rows of carmine lip gloss, ostrich feathers, top hats, tiny bejewelled tutus. The smell of greasepaint, chalk dust, sweaty costumes, damp, dusty dressing rooms.

Alice goes over to the radiogram, finds an old record and puts it on. She sits on the pink over-stuffed sofa lost to Candida, Camden and the dreary 1990s. Candida kisses her on one cheek, leaves quietly and makes her way softly down the carpeted stairs.

There is no light in her window, the curtains are still drawn. Candida hesitates, she is worried about what he is doing in there, but doesn't want to see him, deal with him. She doesn't want to have to face situations she can't control. Besides, she wants something for herself. Uther! He could be all hers, well maybe. She goes in search of Uther. She needs warm, solid arms around her.

She tramps the main road, the traffic is sparse, it must be the middle of the day. The leather on her boots is wearing thin; she can feel the left one letting in cold water. The rain seems to have stopped but the heavy black clouds threaten another downpour. She hasn't seen any clients this week and the money is running low. She blesses the woman who taught her to read the cards, they give her money to buy pretty things when she sees them, to pay the bills and stop her having to be too careful. Clients come by word of mouth, they'd built up over the years and appear in a steady trickle.

Sometimes she did the festivals or sat in the park and waited for people to be drawn by the bright red, green and gold cards. Almost everyone is interested; some people are afraid, as though the cards themselves hold a kind of malevolent occult power and can do wicked things. But the power isn't in the cards, it is in the reader. They just highlight things she already knows. People's eyes read like books, and their fingers, you can't disguise blunt coarse hands or slim delicate ones, nervous hands criss-crossed with lines, fleshy liverish ones, meat eaters' hands.

When she feels bad no one comes, having a man in her flat changed its energy, clients stayed away. Or paradoxically when she really needed work and worried about how she was going to pay the bills, nothing happened. She had to unwind and be almost indifferent for the doorbell to ring constantly. She carried her cards with her, just in case, and her crystals – amethyst, rose quartz, turquoise.

She thinks about Uther, could she dream up a future with him? A cottage with roses? She can see the cottage, and her and the panther, but Uther seems to be around the corner, out of sight, just popping out.

Disconcerted she hurries through the High Street, dodging and weaving bus queues, wandering drunks, mothers with pushchairs, old people tottering unsteadily, teenagers standing in groups. It is a long walk when you are in a hurry, she is puffing and sweat breaks out on her face. She stops to catch her breath, and walks more slowly into the tree-lined street which leads to Primrose Hill. This street is always dark, foreboding, as though it has a malevolent secret life. High three- or four-storey houses with wide balconies and white stone steps leading to the front door, pillars either side holding up the first-floor balcony. High, wide windows, window boxes, velvet curtains, even a rocking horse in one. She doesn't take this route often, feels it is bad luck and wishes she'd gone the other way, via Chalk Farm. The road branches and she takes the right fork walking beside the railings on Primrose Hill. She sees the bus rise up in the distance and her heart beats faster.

She won't exactly apologise to him, just make amends somehow.

She is sorry she lost her temper; that was one of the things people found repellent, men especially. Well, she usually only got angry with them. She tries a smile out, it feels a bit sickly. An old man passing her in the street looks at her strangely. She bursts out in embarrassed laughter, blushing beetroot.

When she arrives, the bus seems empty. She taps on the door, waits but there is no reply. She bangs harder and then harder, but nothing. She looks around but the street is deserted. Heavily she turns homewards. No one is there. Why had she expected that there might be?

She stops at a posh café and orders a plate of apple cake and a mug of steaming, foaming cappuccino. The waitress eyes her coldly and brings her food. She eats, looking out disconsolately on the late afternoon. She feels a listless desolation seep into her. She catches her face in the mirror, her nose glows red, her whole face is flushed and sweaty, the bruise livid. She sits back in the spindly gold chair. She orders more apple cake and eats without tasting. Dabbing her lips on the napkin she gazes vacantly ahead, sated, dowsed, leaden.

She sees a figure pass the window and realises with a start it is Uther. She jumps up, the chair falls backwards and clatters on the terracotta floor. The assistant rises startled as she yells his name and breaks into a run. A hand tugs at her, she opens her purse and, taking out a note, presses it into the hand. She calls his name, the man turns around, it isn't Uther. Humiliated she stops and, standing on the pavement, tears stream down her face. The assistant smirks, passers-by hurry, faces look away. She stands gulping, shuddering, not sure where she is or what to do. Finally, she turns her face into the wind and walks slowly back towards home.

Chapter Twenty-Eight

☾

She feels the panther nuzzle her hand. He brings her to her senses. She turns around and in the driving rain walks on to Primrose Hill. The hood of her cape slides off and she shakes her head, releasing her heavy red hair. She begins to run and she and the panther climb the hill.

At the top the February wind has daggers drawn. Gusts of icy air fresh from Siberia pull and tug her clothes, her hair, her earrings. They reach the summit. The bushes, gnarled and black bare, quiver, the grass flattens. Then the wind calls a dirge.

She reaches the top, driven back by gusts from behind her, to the side, in front. Standing at the wide, flat summit Candida opens her arms out wide and screams and screams and screams. She screams frustration, screams pain, screams anger. She screams for the boy, for lonely Alice, for Bill, for Uther and his fecklessness, for the bloke and his empty heart. She screams for the mess and the filth, the lies and despair, for the hope and the dreams, she screams and screams until she feels her heart will burst.

The wind stops. A stillness falls. There is a clear quiet as though the wind has heard her, listens and is waiting. She feels a surge of power; energy charges through her. Across the hill she sees the city. White and yellow lights glitter; a long, grey bank of cloud envelops the high buildings. She feels its energy, a many-headed hydra, tentacles reaching and penetrating. She sees the faces of children in shop doorways, pinched with the cold, begging monotonously, hope-less. She sees the wealth, the glittering, exuberant, extravagant, cornucopia of colours and smells. Gilded pillars, marble; soft, deep velvet; sparkling, spinning crystals. She sees tables groaning with food from all places, lobsters, pawpaws, sweet avocado; she sees a hungry man poking through the rubbish bin, finishing a half-eaten sandwich, drinking a discarded Coca-Cola.

The children on the streets selling, fixing, sniffing, smoking. She sees beauty in the dawn, a falling leaf, a Leonardo, hears a madrigal. She sees them all mixed. The sacred and the profane struggling in the beast to survive, to breathe, trampling one over another, small shoots trying to reach the light, tall trees to stay there.

She sees the city change, become a forest, a Roman town, a medieval village. She sees smoke rise and flames lick and destroy and masons build again and bombs fall burning, shattering and it growing glass and chrome, taller, bolder. She sees the falling and building and falling and building, impermanent, cocksure, then doubtful, then faithless, the people drawn along, swarming, surging over its rooted boundaries.

Hope. The fragile small dreams, ephemera, urgent desires and the things that last, the timeless beauty of a painting, incandescent sound of human song, a curved arch of smooth white marble, a splendid spreading chestnut tree, tended, cared for.

The beauty remains. The swarming masses rising and falling, growing and shrinking. From the hill she sees all this, feels around her older spirits who watched the city emerge from the swamp and grow raucous, fall and grow again. The spirits of the trees and the land watch patiently as the city struggles between hope and despair to pull itself from the swamp, the marshes, and reach boasting to the skies. The elderflower, the oak, hawthorn and copper beech stand, while the earth turns, millennia passing, and the wind waits. A gust passes her face, she feels a presence, something light, pure and old, an ethereal hand on her shoulder. She knows, at that moment that none of it matters, none of it.

A small patch of blue appears in the leaden sky, duck-egg blue, a watery sun streaks the dark cloud. There is a holding and a waiting and the spell is broken. The sound of traffic seeps through, the sun slides away, Candida gently lowers her arms. She crouches down with the panther, holds him close, his big head nestling on her knees, purring, twitching his whiskers. She picks him up and spins him around and around. He jumps away and they walk together over the brow of the hill and into the city.

She crosses the little bridge over the canal. Barges are moored there, brightly painted red and green, brassy floral patterns, they sway and bob gently nudging the water, black and thick like petroleum. Wisps of smoke come from a stove pipe, a dog pads along the towpath, ducks swim past, green-brown backs catching an oblique light and shimmering.

The branches slicked with rain dip, the falling drops catching in puddles, brief ripples. A faint river mist is rising, massing where the canal curves away. A grey dense cloud of water vapour hangs over the dead vegetation, old nettles bare and spiky, grass more black than green. A bird flies up from the undergrowth and calls a lament, its mate choruses deep in the trees. Freezing air exhaled in puffs of steam, they walk toward the flat green of the park. A solitary runner, mud-splattered, weaves a steady path through the mire at the boundary hedges. The sky is darkening, a yellow light mixed with the slate grey and makes a bruise lying low over London rooftops. It has a brooding quality and muffles the noise of the traffic crowding the streets for the homeward crawl.

Like the runner she follows the boundary and, squelching ankle deep in mud and dead leaves, walks around the perimeter; her feet slide in icy water which soaks the leather of her boots. The wind picks up mercilessly, whips through the branches, ripples across the high grass, wrenches her clothes.

She stands by the mosque. The golden globe dull in the darkening light. Through windows she can see the glittering ceiling with a million crystals. The slim minaret topped with the crescent moon is empty, dark bushes surround its entrance. She walks around, past the pillared whiteness of Nash's terrace, high windows, tall ceilings, works of art, sleek limousines; space and beauty. Crossing, she finds the rose garden barren and the black swans sleeping; ducks and moorhens swim in groups and the white swans in ruffled feathers call to one another across the great lake.

A splash of colour in late-planted beds, red-berried bushes crouch low with yellow variegated and satin leaved shrubs, red and silver fruits. The bandstand empty, all the deck chairs put away. She walks to the theatre, looks but there is no one there. Sits on a hard wooden bench outside the deserted café. Coarse rosemary grows in one corner. She takes a leaf, rubs it between her fingers, inhaling pungent camphor.

She leaves the park and wanders the back streets of Fitzrovia, along Titchfield and behind the crumbling hospital across into Soho. She sits in the square a while, contemplating the worn statue, then moves down, threading and weaving through homegoing crowds. Into Chinatown, smelling foreign smells, strange foods, flattened, red-skinned ducks, trays of exotic fruits nestled with vegetables that have no English name. In Leicester Square she watches the clock, mechanical cows and milkmaids chiming the hour. Through the little park and across the busy clogged road she sees the dome on the opera house, the church of St Martin in the Fields.

Trafalgar Square is empty save for a lone tourist wrapped in polythene. The pigeons race in groups, swooping and diving they nest in the eaves of the great houses of South Africa, Canada. Open-topped tourist buses, bright blue, juxtaposed with the pillar box red of the routemaster and some an anaemic green, fight for space in the jammed road. The lions, shit-streaked, bored and disdainful, watch as she crosses the square and walks under the arch. Some queen, some battle, its memory faded; a great arch embellished in a millennia dead language. Ahead the ugliest barn in London but no flag.

The park, the tamest of London, another ribbon of black water, she queues to buy scalding tea and sticky buns from a stall at its entrance as night falls, crosses into Petty France and into the great Westminster. Square-arched, fake-gothic, pock-marked buildings. A motorbike roars and she is on the other bridge between north and south and can see the Oxo tower, the slab of hospital and barge lights lit, speeding across and down the river. Lights in the House burn and blaze and Candida leans over the swirling water, panting hard.

She is drawn by the swirling water and feels the gravity pull. She longs to merge like Ophelia with the artery of the city, unravel herself to the fierce tides and be pulled effortlessly to salt marsh and the open sea. She imagines a flaming barge set alight with pitch tapers at four corners, wind catching the hemp sail and pulling at the knotted figure as the flames lick deeper, exposing crisped flesh and sinew. She sees gunboats and schooners returning from the Indies with cinnamon and cloves, chocolate of the Incas and indigo, gunpowder, the finest silk, white ivory.

Hulks carry refugees, and half-dead slaves, a traffic in people, Danes, French, Dahomey, Russians, Hugenots, Jews from Poland, Chinese sailors, English Protestants, Irish Catholics, human cargoes. Exotic beasts, the lion, the ape, the scorpion, the black widow crouched in golden bananas. The scented woods, the brandies, ylang ylang and jasmine, saffron and coriander, scented pine wood and dark ebony.

Troop ships to fight the Spaniards, doodlebugs, flying ships, even a rumoured submarine. The body snatchers and the lightermen jostling and barging for a place. The river full of ghosts of ice fairs, smugglers, secret rendezvous. Life blood of the city.

The lights glow on in the Palace of Westminster, warm, golden, safe through mullioned windows, wire mesh to stop bombers, the anarchists are gone, replaced by Celtic furies. Outside rowdy gatherings and rotten eggs, for Cromwell, greedy kings, corrupt politicians. Still the same, power and privilege. She wonders if it will turn to dust, or when.

She feels her life tossed into that black river and sees it whirling, dancing on pockets of air before twisting, falling and floating on a black wave carried downstream before sinking into the thick mud.

She does not cross the river but retraces her steps up and across the city, along St Martin's Lane, where theatregoers mingle with opera crowds and the queue for the cinema snakes into the street. Restaurants gleam, a hundred little cafés with a thousand patrons smoke and talk and sip their cappuccinos, nibble pizza and lick their fingers. She walks along the rows of bookshops, cutting through to Charing Cross Road and walking diagonally in side streets through alleyways, past bus stops and street vendors. She covets silks in the windows and books and paintings and pretty things. Passing her a red bus lumbers; she sees its number and jumps on, holding the pole and leaning outward, hair streaming till the conductor frowns her in. But he cannot suppress a smile, his white teeth gleam, she winks and sits exhausted as the bus trundles and lurches northward.

Chapter Twenty-Nine

In the tunnel Bill slept badly, woke shattered in the late afternoon. It is deserted, except for a small crowd hunched around a burnt out fire, drinking. His body aches, it feels like the temperature has dropped ten degrees overnight, he can see the air misting as he exhales. His nose, fingers and toes are numb, his head feels sodden with damp. He sits upright and coughs and coughs until a lump of phlegm shakes loose, he spits it out, it is bright yellow. He is glad he only has another week to go. His lungs wheeze and groan, he feels a dull aching in his back; the river mist will kill him if he stays any longer.

He stands up and brushes down his coat; it is stained and crumpled from being slept in. He wishes he knew where he'd left his hat. He ties his scarf and without looking back walks into the otherworld.

There is a light fog, the sun a pale yellow blur in the white cloud. Ordinary life passes him at a run, cars speed the roundabout, buses honk, taxis squeal. Men and women in suits and overcoats swarm in and out of the Shell building, briefcases swinging. The flower seller outside the station is swathed in a thick coat, her nose pillar box red. Bill crosses to the sandwich shop and orders tea. The crowd thins around him, smartly dressed clerks and middle managers look alarmed, disgusted. He was going to sit down with his tea, but without asking it arrives in a paper cup, they don't want him staying. He takes it and pays, angry now; his money is as good as theirs. He looks evilly at the queue and hopes they'll all get made redundant soon. No one returns his gaze.

He leaves the shop and stands outside, sipping the hot sweet tea. Its heat slowly diffuses into his body and he feels his heart race. Fired up, he crosses the bridge, moving north. His mind is clear. The boy, what matters is the boy. Vengeance is the act of a frightened man, he'll salvage the living. He climbs aboard the bus and, sitting on the top front seat, wills it to rush through the clogged streets.

He had woken full of dread. Suicide, he might kill himself or he might attack the girl. Coldly he curses his own stupidity at leaving them together. He'd seen the boy kill the dog and enjoy it, would he enjoy hurting her? The bus crawls, the bus creeps, their progress an agony of waiting. Grinding his teeth in frustration he jumps off at Warren Street and takes the tube, waiting an interminable time for the Northern Line.

At Camden he is out. Then, hesitating he takes the route to Uther's bus, if there is trouble he doesn't want to find it alone. Bill looks at the rough map Uther drew last night, and follows the road through the parade of shops into Elsie's street. Walking past her flat he sees an ambulance draw up, they are bringing her home.

Bill feels guilty. He's forgotten all about her. She walks unsteadily between the drivers, dwarfed by them. Bill stops and, shocked by her waxy grey face, slows down. She's shrunk in two days. Become less the puffy, blousey Elsie and more a crone of loose skin and bone. Tufts of unruly hair blow about, she has her slippers on and looks confused when he greets her with a peck.

They help her inside and the kids come down. The flat is spotless, pristine, scent of disinfectant masked by patchouli burning in a corner. The girl beams but Elsie is bereft, looking for the cats and the dust balls, the half-eaten saucers of food, the rancid milk. Bill sits her down and brews a pot, the girl brings a pint of milk and a dozen custard creams but Elsie is not impressed; she looks through them and beyond them, her eyes searching.

They try to undress her and put her to bed, but she lashes out angrily at them. 'Leave me alone! I'm not helpless. Not yet anyway.'

Elsie lies on the bed fully clothed and closes her eyes. The moggies howl and scratch at the window and Bill lets in the first crowd. They swarm around her and settle purring on her chest, her legs, her belly, pinning her down.

Bill is busting to get to Candida's; he is worried about her. He phones Alice who answers in a high-pitched, girlish voice which drops two octaves when she hears Bill's serious tone. Alice says she'll be around as soon as she can; she is waiting for Pat.

Bill sits in the chair and sips his tea. The Hammer Horrors slink out save for the girl, Jacqueline, who sits with him, several questions burning on her tongue. She doesn't ask them but looks up as Uther comes in the room. He opens his arms wide to her and hugs her tightly.

He greets Bill warmly, noticing his fatigue, the grey shadows on his cheeks, his red-rimmed eyes. They sit and eat the biscuits as Elsie snores and whisper commonplaces. The girl shifts in her seat and looks at Uther who looks at Bill who watches the sleeping figure.

Jacqueline and Uther creep out after Bill and stand in the hall whispering. He is kissing her neck, she, worried, pushes him away.

'Pete's upstairs! They'll be down any minute!' She smiles nevertheless.

'When then?' Uther is getting impatient, he doesn't like to have to wait too long, not for sex.

Jacqueline smiles, she'll make him wait a while yet. 'Soon!' she says and disentangles herself.

Uther looks at her and wonders if she is worth the aggravation, he isn't sure. He remembers Bill and forgets about Jacqueline at the same instant. 'See you,' he calls, slamming the door. Outside Bill is waiting for him.

'Sorry I was so long.'

Bill looks at him, wondering whether to say anything, but decides against it. They fall in step and walk slowly to the flat, in silence. Bill is worrying about Candida, Uther thinking about Jane. They neither of them hurry but slowly, heavily, pace out the route, hardly noticing their surroundings.

When they arrive they ring the bell; there is no reply. Looking up they see the curtains open but darkness inside. Bill's feelings of foreboding return. They ring again, but no reply. A sick feeling in his throat, Bill cries aloud from fear and tiredness. Uther, calmer, pushes the other bells and finally finds someone to let them in. They climb the stairs. Bill, half expecting a trail of blood dripping from the door, or smoke or flooding water, is struck by the banality of the chocolate-coloured door, number nine.

They ring again and knock. Silence. A neighbour pokes his bald pate out and asks suspiciously what the problem is. He has a spare key. They let themselves in, the man behind them watching. He's heard music not long ago and dancing or shifting furniture. Greedy for a chance to see the fat lady's flat he sniffs around, nose twitching disapproval. No body. Yet. They check the rooms, kitchen, living room, embers glowing, bathroom, they stop before the bedroom door. Creaking as it opens they see the boy spread across the bed in white satin, breathing softly. Not dead, not yet.

Bill smiles a wintery smile in relief and they creep out again. The neighbour hangs around. They return the key and open the door for him lest he never leave. Uther fixes the fire, which blazes uncertainly, unevenly under the unfamiliar hand. They sit and watch each other and wait. Where is she?

A car hoots outside, they pay no heed. Again, louder, longer, more insistent. Uther looks at Bill as he walks toward the window. Parked in the road is a taxi and outside is Pat, waving frantically. Uther lifts the window; she shouts something he cannot hear and Bill, joining him, says they should go down and see what the trouble is. Fixing the door open they run down the long stairs, but outside, the cab has gone. Baffled they wait; it appears again. She stops and squeals her brakes, she jumps out, they can see there is a man in the cab.

Pat is breathless and clutches at them. 'The man! The man I picked up with the boy! He got in the cab and I recognised him at once! I . . . er . . . locked him in the cab.'

A man, red-faced, is banging and pulling at the door. They move over to watch him, dispassionately curious. The veins on his temples are swollen with rage; he seems to be almost foaming at the mouth; his teeth are sharp and a trickle of saliva dribbles down his chin. His eyes are rather bloodshot. They watch him dumbly as though he is an animal at the zoo, this infuriates him further; he snarls and curses them and pulls at the handle.

A lorry draws up behind the cab, it cannot pass and sounds its horn. Pat jumps in and drives around the block. Bill and Uther wait, stunned. Neither had expected to find the man and have no idea what to do.

'We must talk to him.'

'Talk? He didn't seem that disposed to talk. I don't like this, isn't it kidnapping?'

'Well, what did he do? No, we'll take him inside and confront him with the boy.'

'And what about the boy? Do you think he'll want to see him? I don't think so.'

'Well, what else can we do; we can't just let him go, can we?'

'No.'

The cab draws up again; Pat looks desperate. Uther and Bill tell her to open the doors. Uther at one, Bill at the other, with Pat hovering. The man cowers as the two men enter the cab, now he won't leave. They sit either side of him and Pat locks the doors. The cab pulls off again, the traffic hooting and swearing at her, she drives around for the third time. Uther and Bill tell her to go to a police station. The man calms down and looks coolly at Bill.

'What do you want from me?'

Bill looks at him blankly. What does he want now he has him in front of him? In truth he wants him to go away, disappear off the planet; he wants someone else to decide what to do with him. Bill looks at Uther who shrugs.

'Money? Do you want money?' The man is reaching for his wallet.

'*Money? Money*?' shrieks Bill. 'You think that money fixes it! Makes what you bastards did to the boy all right? *Stuff your fucking money*!'

Tired beyond limit, Bill grabs him by the collar and he looks into those clear grey eyes. 'Animal!' The man blinks and tries to pull away, but Bill is stronger.

They stop. Pat has parked on a piece of waste land, she opens the hatch and looks at the three of them. Bill wants to pull the man out, drag him on to the ground and beat the evil out of him. His fingers are closing around the man's throat.

'Bill!' Uther is worried, he doesn't want to commit murder or watch it being committed. Bill relaxes, the moment passes.

'Well what are we going to do with him?' Pat looks worried, this is kidnapping, she doesn't want to lose her licence.

'We should take him to the police.' The man throws her a look of pure hatred.

'No!' Bill knows that in the hands of the law with an expensive barrister, he'll get off. No, he wants something else, but what?

'Drive back to the house. I want the boy to decide.'

Pat slams the hatch shut and drives on again.

For the fourth time she pulls up outside the flat, this time there is a parking space. She pulls in and turns the engine off. 'Well?'

Bill and Uther get out and drag the man with them. He comes listlessly, his resistance appears to have left him. Bill motions to the open front door and he walks carefully up the steps, Uther and Pat at his sides holding his arms, Bill behind. Uther pushes the front door back and they walk up the stairs.

Suddenly the man wrenches free and Uther and Bill topple backwards. Flattening Pat against the wall, he jumps down several stairs and is off running down the street. Uther gives chase but he is no athlete and soon falls behind.

Running, looking behind him, the man turns the corner into the main road and smashes into the bloke. They both fall back, stunned. Coming up behind, Bill is running, waving his arms and shouting. The man takes off again but the bloke soon catches up with him. He grabs him around the throat and nimbly pulls the man off balance and holds him up against a wall, gripping his neck. He bangs his head a couple of times against the brickwork. The man stops struggling and looks at him, stunned, and for the first time, afraid.

Bill and Uther arrive panting, followed by Pat. The four crowd around the man. The bloke is already going through his pockets. He finds a wallet and takes out a business card, credit cards and a wadge of fifty-pound notes. The man wriggles helplessly, Bill and Uther pin his arms, not noticing the bloke pocket the wallet. The bloke whispers, 'I'll talk to you later.'

Without thinking, Bill knees the man in the groin. He doubles over with pain, groaning. The bloke pulls him back upright against the wall smashing his head against it a third time. Uther crowds in and pushes the man back.

'You bastard, you filthy bastard!'

The man looks through him, a faraway panic in his eyes. They crowd around him, pushing him, poking fingers at him, spitting hatred; Bill wants to bash his brains out, Uther feels sick, only the bloke wants to save him, for another kind of hammering.

'Cool it!' screams the bloke through clenched teeth. A crowd of curious onlookers is watching the show. Jolted to his senses, Bill lets the man go, but stands close by; Uther, ever mindful of his well-being, steps back ready to disassociate himself from the others.

'Why do you do it?' snarls Bill.

The cool grey eyes rest on him briefly, he smirks and, looking up, sees a patrol car draw up. The police sit and watch the crowd, debating whether or not it is worth getting out. A wild panic flashes across the man's eyes. He springs free with desperate force, leaps into the road straight into the path of the big red bus trundling its way down Camden Road. He bounces off the bonnet and is flung like a rag doll down and under the wheels.

The bus skids sideways, a car swerves to avoid it and crashes into the police car. Broken glass and shouting voices. The man is squashed flat, dead. Red fluid seeps on to the road from the back of his head, steam comes from the bonnet of the bus. The driver sits by the side of the road, his head in his hands. Somewhere a woman is screaming and children join in crying. Pat and Bill stand frozen, Uther wants to run, the bloke moves forward to mingle with the crowd which the second policeman holds back; he is talking into his radio.

Behind and in front a wail and tooting of drivers begins. The scream of a siren is heard way back in the line of cars. The bus passengers mill around, talking animatedly.

Several more police cars arrive and they began taking out their notebooks. The bloke melts to the back of the crowd. He moves slowly across the road and climbs on a bus going in the opposite direction. Upstairs the passengers watch the grizzly scene. He surreptitiously counts the notes, cursing his bad luck, bad timing. He had been looking forward to years of blackmail.

An ambulance arrives and the crew walk over to the body. It has been covered by a coat. They kneel beside the dead man and then lift him on to the stretcher. He is wheeled away. The policeman talks to the driver and then, as if trying to remember something, looks around for the friends of the dead man; he cannot recognise them in the crowd.

Alice sees it all from the far side of the road. When she sees Bill and the others she crosses over.

'What happened? Who was he?' Alice asks Bill.

'The man who attacked the boy.'

'The man in the pub.'

Bill and Uther speak together, look at each other, 'What?'

Alice sneaks a look at the face of the dead man peeping from under the coat, she memorises the face to tell Elsie. She looks at Bill, who is looking at Uther strangely. Uther has turned a horrible greenish colour and is walking away. Bill shrugs and looks nervously at the advancing coppers. A policeman stands between them, and the body and, facing them, tells Bill and Alice to get back. Bill goes after Uther while Alice walks away. She waves to Bill but he turns away, she continues on up to Elsie's.

The traffic is backed up all the way to the High Street, hooting and honking. Alice walks slowly, trying to work it all out. What was the connection between the toff and Elsie? Maybe he'd been blackmailing poor Elsie, that would explain all the money in her handbag. But blackmailing her over what? Maybe now Elsie would explain it all to her. Perhaps he'd been forcing Elsie to . . . but she couldn't see it, somehow. Elsie is a tough cookie, Alice can't imagine anyone pushing her around.

It is a long walk. Usually she takes a bus, but there are none passing, still held up by the accident. She crosses the High Street, her legs are giving out. She sees a café ahead, an old-fashioned one, and decides to go in and have a cup of tea and a sit down.

Pat, Bill and Uther walk home in silence. Uther has never seen anyone die, he feels very sick, a cold sweat is sticking to his shirt. One moment the man was so alive, struggling, feeling, full of, well, life. And then nothing, dead meat on the tarmac, juices leaking out. He tried not to see his dead face but was compelled to look. A bland surprise, his mouth open, pink-lined, spittle mixed with blood running out of his nostril. Uther stops and leans over a low garden wall, his stomach heaves and he vomits between the dustbins. The others keep on walking. Uther wipes his mouth and sits on the wall, trying to regain his composure. He feels awful and wants to curl up and cry. He watches the police milling around with terror and keeps looking behind him, afraid they will remember the dead man's companions. He is a murderer, or so he feels. He will never forget those staring, terrified eyes. Never.

Pat and Bill work out their story should the police ask. Pat has seen accidents, dead children, women, old men. The blood always the same, thick tomato, red, viscous, stuck to the ground and blackened. She is afraid for her licence; she knows how little tolerated women cabbies are. She wonders if they scratched the cab bundling him out. She feels content, though, that he died like that and pleased with herself for making it happen. It was only her quick thinking that brought them all together. She knows the boy will be happy, safe now that the man is dead. She looked into his cold eyes just before he jumped, they seemed empty, without feeling, as though there was no one home.

Bill is in a numbed fug. He asked for justice, but wasn't expecting death. He wonders if the man meant to die, but doubts it. He doesn't know if that made things any better. He is shocked at his own violence, thought all that was long gone. Bill had wanted him dead, remembers hitting, kicking, tormenting the man, worse, enjoying it. That is the frightening thing, he'd liked the power, the fear in the man's eyes, making him hurt, he'd liked it. He sees Uther throwing up and feels contempt at this soft boy; he leaves him to it and walks groggily to the flat.

When they reach the house the front door is wide open and Mark, still dressed in white satin, is sitting on the step. His face lights up when he sees them all walking towards him, he thought they'd left him, now he sees them coming home. He's picked up one of the Tarot cards and waves it as he sees them. They flinch when they see it, Death the grim reaper is giving them a bony grin.

Chapter Thirty

The party is in full progress. Her flat is crowded. Bill is in the bedroom showing Mark his magic tricks, Uther and Jacqueline and the Hammer Horrors are smoking in the front room. The fire blazes, the air is hot and smoky, food is piled on the table, someone brought in pizzas which Alice is cutting up, Pat drove down with French bread and cheeses from the market. There are piles of biscuits, Candida has made two cakes; a chocolate and a lemon sponge. The bloke is frying sausages and someone has brought a huge bag of samosas. Elsie is on her feet again and has brought several bottles of gin which she and Bill have been laying into. Bill brought tiny sweet cakes from the Greek bakery, creamy yoghurt and honey from a beekeeper he knows in Clapham. Pat is serving teas and exotic juices. Candida brings in the mixed collection of plates and a jumble of cutlery. The panther sits under the table, watching it all.

Several weeks have passed since the man died. His death was not reported in the papers and the police haven't found any of them to interview, it was a simple traffic accident. No one wants to talk about that day, they want to forget.

The bloke uses the money from the wallet and the credit cards to lay his hands on a nearly new nicked car which he has all loaded up ready to drive down to Spain. It is the stroke of luck he's been waiting for and he is off straight after the party.

Uther has finally talked to Jane and they have decided to sell the bus and go their separate ways; Bill knows a man who has a friend who was looking for a bus to carry his children's theatre group around the country. The group has just got a grant, so Uther and Jane are paid a better price than they might have got elsewhere. Jane is going to Indonesia with a friend, Uther is staying in Bill's old flat until he moves down to Cornwall.

He's never asked Candida to come with him, she's been so busy with the boy. He's waited and waited for the right time and is still waiting. Bill offered him the sofa and he's been glad of it, he is warm for the first time all winter. Bill moved back in, his months in the tunnels over. He has dreams of adopting Mark and bringing him up as his own. They are slowly building a relationship. The boy is very wary but is beginning to trust Bill. He is still in deep shock and won't leave the flat. Bill and Uther try to coax him out, but he is too scared, even though they promise to be his bodyguards.

Mark wants to stay with Candida. He likes Bill but doesn't trust him in the same way he does Candida, who treats him like a mum without fussing too much over him. She is teaching him how to cook, they've made pastry and he's helped decorate the cakes for the party. She wants him to go to school but he knows once he does the social will find him and they'll send him home or, worse, put him in care. He won't go and says he'll find other ways of getting an education, besides he can't concentrate, he's still very jumpy.

Mark is waiting for the flies to return. He's not had an attack since he threw the tin at Candida, but doesn't expect it to last and is waiting, dreading what he might do. He has tried to tell Candida but he doesn't know how to explain them without seeming completely nuts. He is afraid she might throw him out, he sweats at night worrying about it. Every morning he wakes up quiet in the head he relaxes, until he starts worrying about the next night. He has bad dreams; sometimes he cries out and she comes and sits with him or makes him cocoa and talks until he falls asleep. They tell him the man is dead, but he thinks they are only saying that to cheer him up. He doesn't go out in case they get him again, he said that once to her, but she laughed at him so he keeps quiet. But when she is out he sits by the window watching the road just in case.

Alice comes in for tea and a chat. He can tell she doesn't trust him. She watches with her sharp eyes as he cuts the bread or carries the teapot to the table. Usually he leaves them to it and goes into Candida's room to listen to music. He knows she is talking about him because after she leaves Candida watches him nervously when he handles knives, sits with her back to the wall, until she forgets and becomes her usual self.

Alice's friend Pat also comes round. She is more fun. She promises to teach him how to drive when he is a bit older and tells him jokes she's heard. She goes soppy when Alice comes too and looks at her all misty-eyed. Alice, Pat and Candida have long whispered conversations which stop when he comes into the room. He guesses they are talking about what to do with him. Pat was in a home (her mum didn't want her), and argues with them when they suggest they should tell someone he is here. She even offers to adopt him, but supposes she is too old as well as being bent (which is how she puts it); they'll never allow it.

He wants to stay where he is but expects he'll have to go some time; he is holding out as long as he can. Candida never mentions it, but he knows sometimes she wants to be alone. He hides in the corner as best he can but he gets nervous and breaks things, spills things, annoys her while trying really hard not to. Sometimes he'll lock himself in the bathroom and cry, he doesn't like people to see him weeping. Mostly, though, they get on really well. She is lonely too. He sees her looking at Uther and knows that after he's been around she'll cry in her room and be miserable all next day. Uther doesn't seem to notice. He'll be jolly and friendly or quiet and play his music, but he doesn't notice how gooey she goes when he is around. He doesn't like Uther. He's a fake, he'll flirt with other women, right in front of her.

Uther is doing it right now with Jacqueline even though she is sitting there with her boyfriend, who seems too stoned to notice. Candida is watching red-faced, she looks like she is about to explode. Suddenly, she gets up and her plate drops on the floor. Cake falls softly on the carpet and Candida steps on it as she runs to the bathroom. No one notices. Except Mark. He follows her to the bathroom and knocks on the door.

'Candy, are you there?'

Silence.

'It's Mark, are you okay?'

The door opens. She won't look at him, but he sees she's been crying. She walks past him into the bedroom. He follows her and closes the door. She sits on the bed, crumpled. She looks old. For the first time he sees the grey hairs growing out of the henna. Her mascara is smudged, her face, dimpled, looks swollen, puffed up. He watches her. She looks dully ahead and then sighing, slowly gets up, smooths her dress down and turns her face to the mirror. With a finger she wipes the smudge off and puts some more lipstick on. She stands for a long time looking at her face, her body, her hands. Then turns around and walks into the front room.

The party is in high spirits. Bill and Elsie and Alice have finished off the gin and are showing off their routine, giggling, puffing, red-faced doing high kicks, they've even rolled back the carpet. Uther and the boys are providing the music, while Pat is keeping time with a spoon on the empty gin bottle.

When Candida slips out of the flat no one realises; the sound of the closing door is masked by their raucous singing. Uther and the boys have been smoking all day and are out of their heads. He is sitting next to Jacqueline who is smiling, his leg pressed up against hers, from time to time he leans over to whisper something in her ear, he wants to kiss her more than anything, and she is crazy for him, he can see it, it is only a matter of time. Luckily, the boys are playing tonight, he is wondering if he can spirit her away for an hour or two; she is wondering the same thing.

Pat watches Alice and Elsie dancing. She has fallen in love all over again with Alice and wants her. She imagines undressing her, making love, waking in the morning beside that soft white skin, kissing those pink lips. She shifts uneasily on the chair; she wants a drink and knows she can't. It is a long time since she's been around booze, years in fact, and she feels the old longings. Just to get blotto and not to have to feel what she is feeling, it is too uncomfortable. God she wants her! She should have all those years ago, there were moments when Alice, after too many drinks, had looked at her sideways, coquettishly, but Pat was afraid; she might scare her away. She needs to talk to someone quick but she is rooted in her chair, afraid to break the spell. She watches them dancing and giggling with a sick lightheadedness and wishes she was anywhere but here.

Bill starts dancing with Elsie. He is holding her waist; she's put on some weight after being in hospital and now is a lovely handful. He's been calling round regularly to check she's recovered. She's changed. They haven't spoken about what happened but Elsie has lost ten years and has her old sparkle back. She seems more alive but also graver, more serious. She's given a lot of the cats away and is talking about finding a better place to live, somewhere warmer with central heating, and maybe a garden. Alice is looking out for her, her doctor has written a letter to a housing charity. Her flat is immaculate again and she has started having people round to tea. For the first time in years Bill feels he wants a woman, this woman. He holds her tight as they dance around the room. Dare he kiss her? He is drunk enough.

Elsie is pissed, pissed as a rat. Her dying like that has given her a new lease on life. After the shock had worn off. When she first came home she was shattered and just lay on her bed feeling sorry for herself. But when Alice came with the news the toff had been run over she'd leapt up and danced for joy. Alice told her deadpan and waited flinching for Elsie's explanation. Elsie thought she'd spare her old friend and kept mum. She felt free, she'd escaped.

Alice is drunk too, she isn't used to spirits, they make her quite flushed. She feels really giggly and is so happy that Elsie is okay. She'd been afraid she was going to die, she'd miss her friend. And Pat too, she is like her own kid. Yes, she is so happy.

The bloke sits at the table eating sausages. He calls Mark to come and eat too; he knows the boy is always hungry. Mark is standing watching the noisy mob, standing back like he used to, not sure if he wants to join in and not knowing how to in any case.

Mark sits down; the bloke finds a clean plate and shares out the fat, pink porkers. They eat in silence, spreading pickle thickly on them, eating the white bread the bloke had bought. They eat four each and sit back. Mark gets some tea, strong and from the pot and stirs in five spoonfuls of sugar. The bloke watches him eating; he remembers being that age himself, in a home. Thin, scrawny, bullied by the other kids. The head was a weird old man, touching them up when he could, managing to walk in the showers, watching them. He'd not been interfered with, thank God, but the boy in the next bed, who had a sweet girlish face, was regularly taken away during the night and would come back later and cry himself to sleep. He'd remembered that, he'd blocked out so much, and the boy brought it back. Like pretending to be so tough and inside wobbling like a jelly. He'd tried to show him, without words, that he needed to get hard, to develop his body so they wouldn't push him around, even offered to take him out running, but the boy was too scared to go out. They'd done some press-ups, when she'd gone out, but he was a pansy, more interested in cooking than learning how to be a man.

Mark eats mechanically. The sausages taste like sawdust. He thinks he'd be a vegetarian if it were up to him. He watches Uther with hatred; he is pulling this bird, and Candida has gone out and no one has noticed. Parasites, they'll eat her food, take over her flat, but they don't care about her. The old crocks making fools of themselves, he watches Bill kiss Elsie on the cheek and Elsie look up at him giggly and girlish. He sees Pat watching Alice like she is breakfast. He feels sick, sick of all of them. It is all sex, horrible, filthy, sex, sex, sex. Better to sell it than to behave like this; he watches them disgusted. Bill isn't so bloody spiritual after all, just an old tosser, and Uther, who is so warm and open and friendly, screwing anything that moves, and Pat looks like a wet-knickered teenager, pathetic. At least the bloke is okay; you know where you are with him, none of this sex crap.

The bloke is looking at him funny. He looks down and sees he's been holding the red bread knife and squeezing the blade. It has cut into his fingers; blood is dripping out on to the plate mixing with grease and pickle. He drops the knife, it clatters on the plate. The noise catches the attention of Uther and the singers, they falter; Bill lets go of Elsie's waist and Alice straightens her hair.

They all look at him. He stands up and wipes his face, smearing blood across his cheek. The room falls silent. He looks at them, full of hatred.

'Bastards . . . bloody bastards!'

Silence.

He picks up the red knife again and stabs it down and down and down into the table top. No one moves. 'You don't care . . . any of you! She's gone and no one noticed . . . Bastards!'

Everyone looks around. They don't know who he is talking about, until they count heads and realise that Candida is missing.

'Where is she?' asks Bill.

Uther gets up, seemingly concerned. Someone goes into the kitchen, someone else the bedroom, Pat checks the bathroom. She has gone. The party begins to break up, people are murmuring about the time. Mark springs up and stands in front of the door, blocking it.

'No one leaves, no one leaves 'till she comes back!' He holds up the knife threateningly.

A *frisson* of fear. They group together, only the bloke remains seated; he is smirking; the boy has read his mind; he'd been thinking what a gross lot they were when Mark sprang up. Serves them right. He'd noticed the fat cow leaving and seen what was going on between Uther and Jacqueline. People thought he was thick, but he was sharp, dead sharp.

'Look here . . .'

'Mark, don't be silly.'

'Come on, we've got a gig.'

'Mark, let us out; this is crazy.'

'Fuck off the lot of you. You think you're so great. You're shit that's what you are . . . shit! You,' pointing at Bill, 'you think you're so bloody spiritual, don't you, you stupid old fart, pretending to be on the street, conducting your poncey social experiment, who the fuck do you think you are? Look at you groping Elsie and her loving every minute.'

Bill looks away, Elsie shakes her head as if to brush off his words. She sees Jacqueline smirking. 'And you, pretending to be all nice and neighbourly to me when what you really want is my flat so you can have the whole house. You know her dad owns it, don't you?' She addresses the crowd.

Jacqueline stands up, white-faced, Uther moves away from her. 'Oh, *you*! *You've* got a nerve ... what about the boys then, Elsie, and deals on wheels, Elsie? Tell them how you've been supporting your habit, Elsie!' Jacqueline has seen Elsie's comings and goings.

All eyes turn to her.

Elsie blanches. 'I don't know what you mean, you lying tart! Living with one man and knocking off another, you're no better than I am!'

Jacqueline looks at Uther and her boyfriend, then flushes guiltily. The two men face each other coldly.

'I can explain ...'

The boyfriend stands up unsteadily. 'You bastard ...' He swings a punch and catches Uther on the jaw who reels, falling backward against a chair.

Jacqueline watches, smiling, she has never had two men fighting over her before.

Elsie comes up to her and pushes her. 'You bitch, you're enjoying this. You're nothing better than a whore.'

'Don't you push me around ... Tell them what you did with the boys ... Tell them ... He might have been one of them.' She points to Mark.

Mark goes white and walks slowly up to Elsie. He is shaking, and says in a low voice, 'Tell us Elsie, tell us about the boys.'

Everyone turns to look at her. 'I don't know ...'

Uther says softly, 'The man in the pub, Elsie. How did you know him?'

'He was the same one that got run over, I told you,' says Alice.

'I'm glad he's dead,' Elsie whispers. 'They knew what they was doing ... promise ... they didn't do anything they never did before. He said they would be taken care of ... I didn't know what he was going to do ... I needed the money ... until I saw the dead one I never knew.'

'The dead one? Where?'

'When I died I went to heaven ... and I saw his face there with my mum's and auntie's. His face . . . I see it in my dreams all the time . . . it's driving me crazy . . . I can't sleep.'

'She's not sorry, she thinks they deserved it,' Jacqueline screams. Uther and her boyfriend are bearing down on her.

The boy comes up closer. He looks at Elsie's eyes – sneering, he waves the knife. She looks at him, trying to appear frightened but she reckons they'll get him first. Her cold eye watches his feverish dark one, no one moves. Then he pushes her away disgusted, she loses her balance and falls back onto Bill.

'Trash!' Mark spits. 'It's you lot that's trash . . . I'd never do that for money, it makes you a lousy fucking pimp.' Bill holds Elsie up, he looks stunned.

Alice pushes past the boy and goes to Elsie, crying. 'Elsie, Elsie, it's not true, is it? Please say she's lying.'

Elsie looks at her, hard-eyed. 'It's true, Alice, I needed the money. I got the boys, but I didn't think . . . when I saw him in the pub with another one, I flipped. I couldn't do it any more . . . I needed the money,' she appeals to Alice weakly. 'I had to buy the stuff . . . it nearly killed me.'

Elsie cries real tears for herself, not for the boys. Alice and Bill sit her down. Pat stands rigid, the sound of Elsie's crying cuts her like a knife.

'What stuff?' she asks moving forward. Elsie shrinks back into Bill.

'Coke,' says Jacqueline. 'She's a bloody junkie. Landed her in hospital.'

'What do you know about it, you stupid middle-class bitch? What do you know about life, my life . . . ? I was in pain, I hurt so much.'

'Why?' said Pat, not wanting the answer.

'I had to . . . I had to give up my baby.'

'Why?' Pat's voice is cold, deadened.

'In 1941. I was only a kid, the bastard dumped me.'

'What happened to the baby?' She hears her heart pounding in her ears.

'It was a little girl.'

'*What happened to her?*'

'Where did you dump her or did you sell her off too?'

'No! I made sure it was all legal . . . they took her away directly she was born, hardly let me see her.' She walks across the room and picks up her jacket.

The Hammer Horrors open the door nervously. 'We're leaving. Kid, you know where we live, come round when you want.' Jacqueline files out with them, her head hung; she doesn't return Uther's farewell.

Uther rubs his face and sits down at the table with the bloke. He smiles ruefully, but the bloke remains deadpan. Lost without an audience, Uther deflates, 'Well, I think I'll head off home.' Everyone ignores him, he slinks out.

Pat stands by the door, hugs the boy and leaves.

The bloke gets up from the table and begins collecting his things, no time like now. He wants out of this mess, these people. He finds his bag and fills it with a few things, he puts his winter clothes to one side for the boy and slips a tenner in the pocket of a shirt. He finds the scarab and puts it in with the money; it has brought him luck. Without saying anything to anyone he walks out of their lives. They hear his car start up in the street, it drives off, followed by the hum of the taxi.

Bill looks at the boy. He is rigid, standing clutching the knife. Bill wants to reach out to him but doesn't know how. He smiles weakly, the boy looks away in disgust. Alice and Elsie are putting on their coats, Alice thinks about clearing up the mess but doesn't have the heart. She and Elsie leave, walking stiffly; they both feel their age.

Bill looks at the boy but he turns on his heel and walks into the bedroom. The door slams shut. Slowly Bill moves around the flat picking up plates and glasses. He has his hands in the washing-up when he hears Candida come in. She stands watching him bent over the suds.

'I'll do that, Bill, it's okay.'

He turns round and looks at her. Her mascara has run and smudged; she looks like a panda, large, soft, vulnerable. Bill wipes his hands on his trousers. He doesn't know what to say to her either. He looks helplessly and she shrugs. He walks past her, takes his coat and without saying goodbye goes out of the flat.

She takes off her cloak slowly and walks round. Cups and plates are balanced on the mantelpiece, fallen on the floor, half-eaten food is scattered on the table. She steps on something hard; it is the red knife. She bends down to pick it up. There is blood on the blade and more on the white tablecloth. Dully she looks around for the boy. The panther emerges from under the table and rubs its head on her thigh, his long, heavy tail moving from side to side. She strokes his silky fur and absentmindedly scratches his ears. There is movement from the bedroom; the boy has stayed; of all of them he is the only one who has stayed.

The room is a jumble of smoke, food and left-over ghosts. She crosses to the window and flings it wide open to banish them. The fire is almost out; she stirs the embers and throws a paper plate on them. It catches and burns lopsidedly, giving off acrid black smoke; the food bubbles and fizzes until it is burned. She picks some coals and drops them around the dying flames, pokes sticks of kindling into the red embers. She lights some sandalwood and sets it to burn in one of the pot plants; and a blue candle, which she puts on the table.

She sits down heavily. The cake is only half-eaten; she cuts a slice and slowly, carefully, eats it. Then piece by piece crams in the rest. The boy comes out of the bedroom and stands by the table. He watches her eat the cake; she is facing the door. She looks up and between mouthfuls, smiles at him. He sits down carefully, facing her, and smiles back. He starts on the pile of samosas, they grin across the the mountain of food, and silently, methodically, work their way though it.

Also of interest:

Drusilla Modjeska
The Orchard

'As I watched Clara and Ettie that afternoon, protected by the shade of the verandah from the glare of the sun that illuminated them, it was as if, just for that moment, past and future stood outside each other and unsettled my own present. I saw myself as a young woman proud with grief, and I saw myself strain towards the peace, or calm, of age. It was a moment in which the complexities of my life were poised between both possibilities, as brightly lit as the silhouetted figures I observed. From my vantage point between them, in the borderline of becoming between youth and age, it was the shape of a woman's life that I considered . . .'

In this superb literary novel, notions and memories, fiction and reality float moodily together and spread. In a world of real and imagined dangers, and a climate of hostility between men and women, how does a woman grow into her own life? How does she place herself at the centre of her own story? What is the nature and potential of her power? *The Orchard* is an exquisite and dangerous, risk-taking book about the terms of feminine agency.

'A beautifully written narrative, turning on the stories of four women at different ages, and through their self-analysis, the story of many more . . . *The Orchard* is written with style and complexity.' *Melbourne Times*

'Certain to inspire those who read it to act upon their dreams . . . As enriching a book as you're likely to read.' *Herald Sun*

Fiction £7.99
ISBN 0 7043 4514 5

Stevie Davies
The Web of Belonging

**'The woman writes like a dream.'
Marcelle d'Argy Smith, *Independent***

'Jacob is my wall; my rock. I have not encountered the solidity of this truth until now. Jacob was there, a quality of my being; a rootedness, a quiet.'

Jess has lived peaceably in Shrewsbury with her husband Jacob for many years. He is solid, dependable, beautiful to her. She is contented to be his wife, to look after his elderly mother, aunt and cousin, to be a pillar of their family and community. Then, suddenly, everything changes.

Now Jess must question the entire basis on which she has lived so many years of her life. Must discover whether the identity she has created has really been so valuable to herself and to those around her, and whether there is a different – angry, passionate, fulfillable Jess – waiting to get out.

The Web of Belonging is Stevie Davies' sixth novel – a hilarious, moving, astute and tender book by one of the most respected and acclaimed novelists of our time.

'A poignant, funny and luminous story . . . Davies has written an immensely enjoyable novel, lit by comedy and wisdom . . . One of the funniest, most poignant novels I have read this year.' Helen Dunmore, *The Times*

Fiction £6.99
ISBN 0 7043 4519 6

Linda D Cirino
The Egg Woman

'I come from a long line of farmers. And farmers' wives. There is a picture of a woman farmer on the sack of corn feed we use that shows the woman just the way I've always seen most farmers, looking down. I don't know what she's supposed to be doing on the bag of feed, but she could be bending her head to some work in the house or in the field, some mending or cooking, tending the children. Every once in a while, just to check the weather, I'll take a look at the sky, see how the setting sun tells the next day's temperature, see if storm clouds will come over before the laundry is dry. Mostly, though, my head is bent over like hers. As far back as anyone can recollect, we have been working the land.'

It is southwest Germany, 1936. A woman, isolated from the events of the world, tends her farm. Her husband is away at war; her children are absorbed in the youth movement. Then she finds a man – a Jew – hiding in the chicken coop. Instinctively, she protects him . . .

The Egg Woman is an extraordinary, beautiful and touching novel about prejudice, integrity, self-knowledge and courage.

Fiction £6.99
ISBN 0 7043 4511 0

Hiromi Goto

Chorus of Mushrooms

Winner of the Commonwealth Writers Prize for Best First Book, Canada and the Caribbean Region

Chorus of Mushrooms is the exquisite story of three generations of Japanese women. Naoe, the grandmother, who has mourned the loss of her life in Japan ever since her family left. Keiko, her daughter, who has changed her name to Kaye and abandoned her Japanese-ness in order to assimilate. And Murasaki, who longs to reclaim the heritage her mother threw away and to forge an identity of her own – to bridge the divide between Naoe and Keiko, while closing the gaps in herself.

Chorus of Mushrooms is a beautiful and resonant novel by an author who has been likened to Jung Chang.

'In the process of re-telling personal myth, I have taken tremendous liberties with my grandmother's history. This novel is a departure from historical "fact" into the realms of contemporary folk legend. And should (almost) always be considered a work of fiction.' Hiromi Goto

'Hiromi Goto has written a chorus of place and family and imagination with such clarity and sensitivity that our tongues rest in awe and our ears feel cleansed.' Fred Wah

Fiction £6.99
ISBN 0 7043 4518 8

Veronica Chambers
Mama's Girl

' "Everyone there was just like you. Professionals. Upper-class women."

'That made me wonder what my mother saw when she looked at me. I wondered if everything about me that she chose to see as being white – my education, my career, my social activities – obscured everything about me that was Black – my family, my community, my mother herself.'

Veronica Chambers is a former editor at *The New York Times Magazine* and *Premiere* and is currently a contributing editor at *Glamour.* She has written for *Essence*, the *Los Angeles Times Book Review*, *Seventeen* and *US. Mama's Girl* is her extraordinarily moving account of her own life and her struggle to maintain her loving connection with her mother through pain, disappointment and dramatic change. It is the story of one young Black woman's transition from poverty and discrimination towards equality and success, through disconnection and distance to powerful, deep relationship.

'Young trailblazer Veronica Chambers applies her keen intellect and critical sensibility to an issue too few Black women have had the courage to explore honestly and openly. *Mama's Girl* is a book we have been anxiously awaiting.' Susan Taylor, editor-in-chief, *Essence*

'An unforgettable testament to the resiliency of the human spirit and the depth of love.' *Booklist*

Autobiography/Memoir £7.99
ISBN 0 7043 4510 2

A. J. Verdelle
This Rain Coming

Her hugely acclaimed début novel

The year is 1963. Young Denise Palms has been called home to Detroit from rural Virginia to keep house. Then she becomes the relentless focus of a magnetic new teacher, and Denise is both distressed and inspired. Soon Denise is torn, not only by her desire to be good and fit in and the conflicting demands of her teacher to pursue an education, but also by the growing tension between her stepfather and her beautiful, indolent elder brother . . .

'Truly extraordinary.' Toni Morrison

'A truly unique and resonant work . . . A. J. Verdelle's first novel resounds, her vibrant prose ringing clear . . . Haunting, at times mystical, this novel has all the dimension and beauty of song. To read this novel is to fall under a spell, to open a window, to fly.' ***Los Angeles Times***

'A particularly accomplished début . . . confident, finely realized and strikingly original . . . consistently absorbing and beautifully detailed.' ***Publishers Weekly***

'Brilliant . . . moving, vivid and amazingly inventive.' ***Newsday***

Fiction £6.99
ISBN 0 7043 4493 9

May Sarton
Crucial Conversations

'Sarton has published over forty books and attracted a large and devoted following . . . [Her] utter involvement with life has always been the wellspring of her art.'
Claire Messud, *Guardian*

On the surface, there was no visible reason for Poppy to leave Reed. They had shared a robust and lively marriage, full of storms and passions. They had comfort and money. They seemed friends. True, she was a frustrated artist in her spare time, but she had more time to spare now, and Reed had built her a studio. Yet suddenly she had gone, leaving a cold and angry note. To her husband and to their closest friend, who had nourished himself on their marriage, Poppy's act was a selfish, destructive desertion. But then, in a series of brilliant, searing conversations, a different truth emerges.

A truth about a woman desperate to exist as an individual. To discover once and for all whether her art was real, or mere therapy. To escape from the trap of wifehood, where a woman can suffocate unless her husband has extraordinary understanding, which Reed did not.

In this classic, exhilarating and acclaimed novel, May Sarton reveals the explosive consequences of a growing individual stifled by a social contract.

'The finest achievement of Miss Sarton's novel-writing career . . . A remarkable statement of understanding one woman's inescapable, inscrutable entirety.' Nancy Hal

Fiction £6.99
ISBN 0 7043 4524 2